THE SPIDER:
SLAVES OF THE LAUGHING DEATH

THE MASTER OF MEN!

SPIDER®

SLAVES OF THE
LAUGHING DEATH

By Grant Stockbridge

POPULAR PUBLICATIONS • 2024

CHAPTER 1
DEATH'S SHINING FACE

THE MAN plunged headlong out of the drug store, into the street. He blundered into a parked car, caromed into the traffic. Someone shouted a warning: taxis screamed to a halt, but the man ran on....

His right hand lifted upward, jerkily but did not quite touch his face. Then he knotted the fist until the knuckles were bone white, and thumped it frenziedly against his skull. A whimpering sound squeezed out between his teeth.

His shoulder hit the door of the tall new apartment building on the corner and the glass jangled discordantly to the pavement. A uniformed attendant whirled indignantly to confront him, and the man's hands reached out and set upon the attendant's shoulders and shook him like a child.

"Wentworth's apartment!" he panted. "In God's name, Wentworth's apartment!"

The attendant stared into the man's face and the indignation was sponged from his own. His cheeks sucked in for a shout he did not utter, and grayness crept under the skin.

"That elevator!" he gasped. "That one, there! Top floor!"

The man freed the attendant and reeled into the elevator. He shot out an arm to the control panel, and as the door slid shut, his face peered back from the dimness of the cage—a face marked by pain, inhuman in its agony. And it glistened, as if the

skin budded with little electric flames—small greenish flames that glowed coldly!

The door slammed and the attendant shuddered. He hurried toward a small corner counter, behind which sat the telephone girl.

"Quick!" he gasped. "Quick! Call Mr. Wentworth's apartment. Tell him… Tell him there's a dead man coming up to see him!"

IN HIS apartment, Richard Wentworth confronted the three men grouped about his hearth. Behind a calm smile, his alert mind was wary. He was accustomed to traps. Life compelled him to walk as cautiously as a soldier in a forest sown with land mines. There was menace in these three men; that much he knew. How and when they would strike was less certain.

He said, deliberately, "So you wish me to join your organization, Hunter, and—"

"The Gotham Hounds!" Hunter boomed from where he posed dramatically before the stone fireplace. He uttered his hollow, professional laughter, and showed a great many teeth.

"—whose purpose, as I understand it," Wentworth continued quietly, "is to capture the Spider!"

"Or destroy him!" It was a second man, Carl Laird, who dropped these words coldly across Wentworth's speech. He was sitting rigidly in a stiff-backed chair, his feet carefully together, his squarish hands set solidly on his knees.

Wentworth threw a glance at him, looked deliberately at Hunter, then at Ralph Warring who rested his hands on the back of his neck in a deep chair with long legs thrust out before him. A leather-cased camera lifted and fell on Warring's chest with his breathing. His eyes were almost closed, unreadable.

Wentworth's smile deepened his mouth corners sardonically. "Professional adventurers and romanticists," he said tonelessly. "Embargoed in the United States by foreign wars, and seeking something spectacular to do—at home for a change."

Baird's face burned dully red, but Hunter's laughter boomed out and Warring dropped his words gently from scarcely stirring lips, scarcely veiling his hostility.

"Well put, Wentworth," he said, "and since we are in strange waters, we need a pilot. Will you lead our crusade?"

Wentworth shrugged slightly. "With appropriate publicity?"

"And pictures!" Warring drawled. He began to unsheathe his camera.

In the hallway, the phone bell whirred faintly, and the shadows by the portiere entrance stirred. From them, there stepped a tall bearded Sikh in a spotless white turban. He glided soundlessly from sight, and Hunter's head swung that way. He watched him out of sight with a slight narrowing of his eyes.

"Strangers are always watched here," Wentworth said casually. "There are others… Hunter, I'll give you your answer straight out. If you had another purpose than hunting the Spider, I might be tempted to join your Gotham Hounds; another more worthy purpose… such as supporting the Spider! You see, I happen to approve of his work, though not always of his methods. He fights… *crime!*"

Baird stood up. The flush lingered on his cheekbones. "He violates the law!" he snapped. "He himself is a criminal!"

5

Wentworth faced him directly, but did not lose sight of the other two men. "You make a general mistake, Baird," Wentworth said quietly. "You regard the law as an end in itself. Actually, the law was created by man to promote and safeguard justice. It is justice, not law, which we should serve. And where law obstructs justice, it should be violated!"

There was a flash of white in the darkened doorway of the hall, and Ram Singh bounded into sight. His dark eyes gleamed with excitement above his beard.

"*Sahib!*" His nasal voice was strong. "*Sahib*, the attendants below say a dead man is on his way to see you!"

Like a rasping overtone of his voice, the doorbell began to whir.

HUNTER AND Baird stared toward the doorway in strained attitudes of amazement, but Baird's right hand moved with a deliberate speed and flipped a heavy-caliber revolver into sight. Warring, his lips smiling, had his camera ready. Wentworth saw this while his mind raced on. Was this the moment when the Gotham Hounds would strike?

Wentworth's voice was easy, smooth. "Open the door, Ram Singh," he said softly, "and let us see this… dead man!"

In a movement of smooth speed, Ram Singh whipped open the outer door and the man with the glistening face flung himself, running, into the room. He stumbled to his knees before Wentworth. His voice lifted in a thin shriek.

"Oh, save me!" he gasped. "My face—save me, Spider!"

Wentworth stared down at the scarred face, shining with that cold glow of tiny, devouring flames. He was conscious of the tense men who flanked him; of the flare of a flashlight as Ralph Warring snapped the tableau with his camera. Was this part of the trap? Perhaps, since this kneeling man had called him the Spider. For a moment Wentworth hesitated; then a sharp oath rasped in his throat. The flesh of the man's face was... *dissolving!*

"Ram Singh! Soap!" Wentworth snapped. *"Jackson!"*

From the dimness of the music room a broad-shouldered man in a chauffeur's uniform sprang into view.

"The laboratory!" Wentworth threw at him. "Ammonium phosphate!"

As Jackson spurted toward the hallway, Wentworth caught the shoulders of the kneeling man. "What happened?" he demanded.

The man struggled against Wentworth's grip. His hands became claws ripped toward his face. Wentworth seized his wrists.

"What happened?"

"A child... water pistol!" the man gasped. "It burned! The drug store... man said you'd help me. You... the Spider!"

His last word was a scream. Convulsively he ripped his wrists from Wentworth's grip, clawed in a frenzy at his own face. He groveled on the floor, ground his face against the hearth. His screams diminished. The flashlight flickered again, and before Ram Singh came back, the man on the hearth was still. Across the prostrate body beside which he knelt, Wentworth looked in turn at the three members of the Gotham Hounds. Hunter's smile was still on his mouth, strained a little; his eyes shone with excitement. Laird's long, serious face was stupid with shock.

7

And Warring, carefully attending to his camera, still had his eyes half closed.

"Now we understand your reluctance, Wentworth," Warring said, amusedly. "Am I wrong, or did that man call you the Spider?"

"I am sure," Wentworth said coldly, "that you have been called other, less honorable names… and with perhaps more truthfulness, Warring. If you take another picture, I shall smash that camera."

He deliberately turned the dead man over on his back, and his face drew into harsh lines. The corpse's face no longer shone. It was gleaming white. The bones of the skull, which alone were left, were as clean as newly scrubbed marble.

Wentworth got to his feet. His fists were clenched at his sides. Were these three men involved in the death of this poor creature on the floor? He had thought the whole thing trickery at that first moment, until he had seen how the man suffered… The druggist on the corner had sent him, the man said. The druggist….

"I think I'll run along," Hunter said jerkily. "You will be busy for a while, and I'll phone you for your answer, Wentworth!" His voice came back from the hallway and an instant later, the door clapped shut, hollowly. Warring laughed, a faint, whispering sound.

"Hunter chose the name of hounds," he said. "I didn't know he meant the yellow kind. Well, Wentworth, what happens now?"

WENTWORTH'S HAND flicked beneath the lapel of

his coat, and reappeared with a heavy, black automatic in his fist. His fingers moved efficiently, checking the loading. He replaced it in its holster.

"I think," Wentworth said softly, "that I shall call on the druggist who sent this poor fellow here. It is just possible that the druggist knows more about the Spider than any of us."

Warring's eyes opened wide. His laughter was openly admiring. "Listen, Wentworth," he said. "Show me some excitement. I don't care whether the Gotham Hounds hunt spiders or rabbits... You're pretty cool about being accused of being the Spider."

Wentworth was striding toward the door, Warring at his elbow. Carl Laird followed more deliberately. His long strides carried him swiftly in their wake.

"It is an old accusation," Wentworth said easily, "and one which honors me. Fortunately, or unfortunately, it is not susceptible of proof... Ram Singh, phone the police and tell them precisely what occurred here. They will find me at the corner drug store... Jackson, I'll need the Daimler at once!"

The splintered glass of the apartment's front door was being swept into a neat pile, but the hands of the attendant were still shaking; his eyes had a strained and wild look. Wentworth thanked him briefly, while his keen gaze searched the street. There were parked cars nearby, but none of them was occupied. The drug store across the street was brightly lighted, and empty of customers. Bob Hunter, leader of the Gotham Hounds, was nowhere in sight.

Wentworth was willing to swear that neither of the two men

with him had had any part in the
death of the man in his apartment;
apparently Hunter had been panic-
stricken. Yet in no other way could he
account for the man coming to him
with his dying strength. The druggist?… the idea was fantastic. Still…

did he represent some new threat of the venomous lords of the
underworld? Some new threat directed at the humanity the
Spider had sworn to protect from crime?

Wentworth was weaving a resolute way through the traffic
toward the drug store. His stride was long and purposeful. At
his side, Warring began to chuckle. Wentworth's head whipped
toward the man, and the chuckling grew louder. Even Carl
Laird's long face wore a broad smile.

"What is so amusing?" Wentworth asked.

Warring laughed out loud. "Hunter was right green, he was
so frightened," he said.

Wentworth frowned. The answer did not seem adequate,
but the laughter seemed to have a curious effect of lightening
the tension in his own breast. Everyone who passed seemed to
wear a wide smile. A taxi driver, in a parked cab, apparently was
shaken by uncontrollable hysterics. Wentworth stared at him,
choked back an oath of amazement. The man's license badge,
pinned to his coat, had an unmistakable, greenish glow!

Somewhere in the back of Wentworth's brain, there was a
cold warning of danger, but it could not penetrate his conscious-

ness. He was aware of something strangely confusing in the situation. He should be worried, be on the alert, and yet he smiled....

Warring chuckled, "Come on, let's call on this druggist friend of yours, Wentworth."

Wentworth nodded, and pushed open the door. It seemed to him, in passing, that the knob and fixtures had a slight greenish glow, but it was unimportant The druggist, in white coat and spectacles, behind the soda fountain, bobbed his head and smiled in a way that was familiar. Wentworth smiled back, strolled toward the man.

"You sent a man to my place," he said equably. "Poor chap with a shining face. I was wondering...."

Wentworth never finished the sentence.

As he smiled pleasantly into the face of the druggist, the man suddenly brought his right hand above the counter and revealed an automatic.

Still smiling, the druggist began to shoot at Wentworth!

CHAPTER 2
BIRTH OF FEAR

DESPITE HIS lulled suspicions, Wentworth was in motion instantly. His leap to the left hurled Laird backward, arms wheeling wildly. In the same movement, Wentworth dived for the protection of the marble soda fountain behind which the druggist stood. It was the only bulletproof barrier in the room.

The druggist's first shot had punched through the spot where

11

Wentworth first had stood. The explosion jarred against his eardrums; made a hundred stacked bottles rattle on their shelves; the crash of breaking glass was musical and thin. The second shot lifted a white dust from the edge of the counter—just above Wentworth's head. Fragments of shattered marble whined angrily, and Wentworth felt a stinging shock across one temple.

Wentworth's automatic flipped into his fist, and his gaze raked across the drug store. Laird was flat on his back near the door. As Wentworth spotted him, he clawed out his gun, rolled over on his belly. Half behind a central counter of stacked cut-rate products, Ralph Warring was fighting to get his camera out of its case. His smile was wide, nervous… excited, more than frightened.

Wentworth's automatic rested lightly in his hand while he waited for Laird to get his gun clear. Out of the tail of his eye, he glanced into the glass cases across the store. They showed a distorted reflection of the druggist. He had a knee on the service portion of the fountain, was leaning forward with his gun to fire straight downward at Wentworth! And Laird's gun was free, was dropping into line!

"Don't shoot, Laird," Wentworth called quietly.

At the same instant, Wentworth sent a bullet scorching up past the edge of the marble counter. It notched out a small semicircle, left white dust in the air… but on the upper side, it ripped loose a hundred tiny knife-like fragments. His showcase mirror showed him the stiffening figure of the druggist, an arm flung up across his face as he tottered backward. Wentworth was instantly on one knee. His second shot scored the top of the counter, shattered the mirror behind the fountain. A stack of oranges bounded with soft little thumps to the floor—and the druggist was no longer in sight. He had dropped to the floor!

Laird was scrambling to his feet, gun still in hand. There was an angry flush in his cheeks, but his eyes were not on Wentworth. They searched the top of the counter.

"I'll keep him down!" he snapped. "Cover the far end of the counter!"

It was not until that moment that Wentworth realized that he had expected Laird to open fire upon him! It had not been a conscious thought, but an expression of his subconscious distrust of the three members of the Gotham Hounds. But Laird had withheld his fire, now was charging to the attack!

Wentworth, bent double, sprinted for the opposite end of the soda fountain.

"I want the druggist alive," he called softly.

THE BLAST of a flashlight flung the whole store into momentary brilliance and Wentworth swore as he checked, gun in hand, to command the opening at his end of the soda fountain. He saw Laird bound to the top of the soda fountain. Laird's gun blasted in the same instant and he cursed violently.

"Trap door!" he shouted. "Behind the counter!"

Wentworth whipped around the counter's end, gained the yawning trapdoor, its steep steps slanting down into the basement. His hand flicked to an electric switch nearby, and lights blazed in the dark pit below. Over him towered Laird, eyeing the corpse that lay sprawled at the bottom of the stairs. Warring's flashlight flickered its mild lightning again.

13

Laird's voice came complacently. "How's that for shooting in the dark? I got the beggar right through the back of the skull!"

He jumped to the floor, started toward the steps, and Wentworth's rigidly out-thrust hand stopped him in his tracks.

"Don't go down there!" he said. "Can't you see there's an orange on that man's back?"

Laird said, incredulously, "An orange! What of it?"

Wentworth shook his head impatiently. "My last shot spilled the oranges. Your shot came quite a while later. That man down there was already dead before the oranges fell. *That man is not the one who was shooting at us!*"

Laird swore. "But it looks like the same man. The same clothing. The same gray hair…."

Wentworth's face was becoming pale. He felt a cold fist closing on his heart. "Yes, it looks exactly the same. But now you can see that no blood flows from that wound, that it coagulated long ago. Now—" Wentworth snapped off the cellar lights—"In fifteen seconds, turn on the light again!"

He leaped down through the opening. His feet hit and he dived to the cover of barrels he had spotted from above. As he got his feet beneath him again, the lights flicked on. In all

14

the cluttered basement, nothing moved... but a window that should have been bolted and barred with iron was hanging open. The bars had been sawed away.

Wentworth swore and sprinted across the basement, pulled himself up through the window. Outside was the pitch blackness of an alley. In it, nothing stirred. There was not even the sound of a motor starting.

The killer had escaped.

Wentworth lowered himself slowly, returned to the dead man on the floor and rolled him to his back. Staring up at him was the same face he had seen a score of times, the same face that apparently had

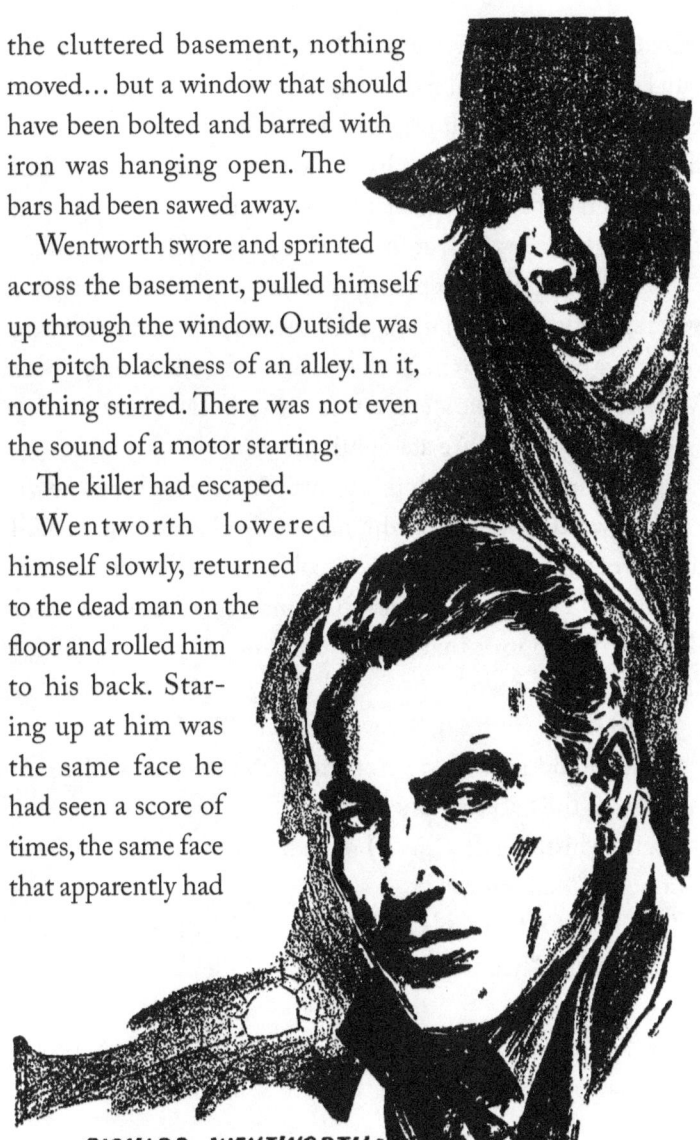

• *RICHARD WENTWORTH* •

15

leered behind that powerful automatic a few minutes before. The gun lay beside his right hand now, a hand that was stained with chemicals. Wentworth frowned, remembering that the right hand that had held the gun had been stained like that, too. But there could be no contradicting the presence of that orange upon the man's back, or the fact that the blood had fully coagulated.

Wentworth cursed violently. He was not a man who gave way readily to his emotions, but this was no second-rate menace he was fighting. Once more that coldness swelled in his chest. When he climbed the steps, it was with a heavy tread.

He said, thickly, "We are fighting… *Munro!*"

Carl Laird frowned at him curiously. "A criminal you know?"

Wentworth laughed. "A criminal who has been reported dead a score of times! One of the most coldly vicious killers in all of crimedom! He has no scruples about mass murder, or any other delicate little horror that will help to line his pockets. God, I thought he was dead!"

Laird shook his head, "I never heard of him."

"You would know him probably," Wentworth said, more quietly, "as the Faceless One." *

Laird whistled softly, "Aye! I remember now! A devil in flesh! But how in hell can you be so sure?"

WENTWORTH NODDED toward the dead man in the basement. "Munro's best safeguard is the fact that no one,

---

* Author's Note: Wentworth's last enounter with Munro was narrated in "The Spider and the Faceless One," in which Munro loosed the horror of fire upon the city.

actually, knows what he looks like. He has a thousand disguises, each one perfect. When he posed as this druggist in order to trap and kill me, he took the trouble even to stain his right hand with druggist's chemicals, as that poor devil below has done through years of work. Only Munro would have thought to attend even to that minute detail. God in heaven! Now, a man can scarcely trust his closest friend, for it may be Munro!" His eyes narrowed. He said softly, "Where is… Hunter?"

Warring was perched on a stool, smiling across the soda fountain at them. "I've known Hunter quite a while," he said amiably. "I don't think he's Munro."

Wentworth smiled twistedly. "I don't think you got the point," he said. "How can you be sure that the man who called with you tonight really is Hunter? You two gentlemen I can exonerate. I saw both of you and the disguised Munro at the same time."

Warring shook his head, casually helping himself to a glass of soda water. "If Munro is as good as all that, couldn't he disguise one of his henchmen, also? No, my dear fellow Hound of Gotham, you can't be sure even of me!"

He set the glass down, and Wentworth took it by the rim, wrapped it in his handkerchief before he thrust it into his pocket. "Fingerprints can't lie," he said grimly. "When I get a set of Munro's prints, I'll compare them!"

Warring only smiled, with his eyes sleepy again, and Wentworth strode sharply from behind the counter, angled toward a telephone booth. He put through a call to police headquarters, and tried to reach Stanley Kirkpatrick, the Commissioner of Police. Kirkpatrick was his personal friend—though he was also, and bitterly, the enemy of the Spider!… But Kirkpatrick had left his office, so Wentworth rapidly reported the shooting to the desk sergeant, then put through another call.

There was a faint smile on his lips now as he listened to the distant whirring of the phone bell. As always, when a new battle loomed for the Spider, he must warn Nita van Sloan, the woman he loved. There was an especial danger this time, with Munro once more up to his demon tricks. The memory of the ghastly face of the dying man who had sought him out wiped the smile from Wentworth's lips, as he heard Nita's gay greeting.

"Listen, dearest," he said rapidly. "Munro is busy again. Yes, Munro! From now on, trust no one at all… least of all, anyone who seems to be me!"

Nita laughed, "But I never trust even you, Dick! So what am I to do now?"

Wentworth frowned, not at Nita's words, but at her gay humor. She, of all people, should realize the danger represented by Munro! She who so narrowly had escaped death under the merciless slash of his private guillotine!

"Nita," he said sharply. "This is deadly serious! Don't you understand? Munro—"

Nita's laughter rang again, and it had a thin, unnatural note. "Munro? Munro? Now, where have I heard that name before?"

Wentworth's fist whitened about the receiver as he listened to the silvery gaiety of Nita's laughter. He was remembering with a sudden fierce intensity the moment just before he himself had entered the drug store. Laughter had been on his lips, a laughter which no man could account for by the sequence of events. A

18

taxi driver had been almost hysterical over nothing at all, and on his lapel, the driver's badge had a greenish glow like the face of the man who had died!

Wentworth's lips tightened. He put hard emphasis into his voice. "Listen, Nita," he said firmly. "Try to listen seriously to me for one moment. On your mantelpiece is an old French clock of brass—"

"What a memory the man has!" Nita cried.

"Look at that clock, Nita!" Wentworth insisted harshly. "Are you looking at it? Good. Now, listen to me. Is there a greenish glow about that clock, as if it had been painted with radiolite paint? Is there, Nita?"

NITA LAUGHED. She made no other answer at all, just that pointless laughter that went on and on. Wentworth fought for control of his voice.

"Please, Nita," Wentworth said quietly. "Are you laughing because the brass of the clock is green?"

Finally, Nita's voice, weak with laughter came to him: "Dick, you must be clairvoyant. You should have told me before. Yes, the clock looks so funny, all shining green...."

Wentworth's voice rasped with sudden fierceness. "Nita, that green glow means that Munro is near you, threatening you! Do you understand? Oh, Nita, listen to me—don't open your door until I come there. Don't—don't wash your face, or touch any liquid, do you understand?"

Nita's fresh laughter vibrated in the phone. "Oh, Dick, I can't stand this! Please let me wash my face. It's very dirty. I've been making mudpies...."

Wentworth struggled frantically to make her understand the peril that turned his heart cold with fear for her, but Nita refused to take him seriously. Finally, Wentworth hung up and left the booth. The pale tension of his face brought Laird sharply to his feet where he sat beside Warring.

"What now?" he snapped.

Wentworth strode swiftly toward the door. "Come with me, if you like, and I'll explain!" he snapped. "No time now!"

The big Daimler was at the curb. There was a police car across the street; plainly the uniformed men had gone to his apartment. A siren was dim in the distance, growing louder. But he could not wait now. He knew that in some unaccountable way, Munro was causing that wild, nonsensical laughter that poured from Nita's lips. He had used the same unaccountable weapon to disarm his own suspicions just before he entered the drug store. And in some way, that faint greenish glow he had noticed before was connected with the mad laughter. If only he could reach Nita in time....

Behind him, Laird called out in a tense voice, "I have my car here. I'll follow with Warring!"

Wentworth nodded, and stepped into the rear of the Daimler. It surged from the curb with lightning acceleration. Wentworth stared at the broad shoulders of the man in chauffeur's uniform behind the wheel, and his lips tightened grimly. He got out his gun.

"Jackson," he said softly. "What were the last words I spoke to you before I left the apartment?"

Wentworth caught the startled lift of Jackson's eyes to the

rear vision mirror, the surprised line of his straight mouth. "You said, sir, 'Jackson I'll need the Daimler at once.'"

"And before that?" Wentworth prompted softly.

Jackson frowned, weaving the car northward. "'Jackson—the laboratory. Ammonium phosphate.'" Jackson's voice sounded mechanical, worried.

Wentworth relaxed, thrust his gun back into his holster. "Good," he said. "Forgive my quizzing you Jackson, but we are fighting—Munro!"

Jackson uttered an oath. "Good God in heaven! Forgive me, sir, but if you'll just tell me—what did you say to Mr. Warring just before you left the apartment?"

For an instant, Wentworth stared at Jackson without understanding, and then he laughed softly. It was justified. Jackson, too, was taking precautions against being tricked by the fabulous disguises of Munro!

Wentworth satisfied Jackson, told him their destination and the urgency of their purpose. The Daimler's motor purred louder with mounting speed. A police whistle blew behind them, but Jackson ignored the summons and raced on. Wentworth's keen eyes flashed at the traffic about them. Munro had made a clean get-away from the drugstore, but even so he could not yet have reached Nita's Riverside Drive apartment. Therefore, he must have previously established whatever hellish device caused that mad laughter. It was entirely possible that Munro might be at this moment on Wentworth's trail! Hunter... what had happened to the Master of the Gotham Hounds, as that impetuous fellow styled himself?

Apparently, Hunter had fled in fright at view of the ghastly new death that Munro had devised; yet that did not fit with the man's reputation as a professional adventurer. Abruptly, Wentworth leaned forward and struck the window glass behind Jackson. The Daimler swerved to the curb, but Wentworth did not alight at once. He was staring toward two men in a dim side street that led toward Broadway. One of those men was a uniformed policeman; the other was—Robert Hunter!

As Wentworth stared, Hunter's fist struck the cop's jaw! Before the policeman had fallen, Hunter had ripped the man's revolver from its holster and was sprinting down the dark side street!

CHAPTER 3
THE TERROR STRIKES!

GRIMNESS SETTLED about Wentworth's chiseled mouth. His hand moved to a button beneath the left cushion and the seat slid forward, revealing a secret compartment—the dressing room of the Spider! Wentworth shook his head. He could not yet be sure that Hunter was the man he sought!

Wentworth stepped to the pavement. "Keep the car close!" he ordered Jackson, and then sprinted after Hunter.

The man had hesitated just short of the lighted marquee of a theatre; the gun was no longer in sight. After that moment's hesitation, Hunter tugged down his hat—and went into the theatre.

Seconds later, Wentworth himself turned into the deserted lobby and crossed straight to the inner doors. Worry over Nita nagged at his mind, but he reassured himself that Munro could not possibly have reached Nita's home. And Hunter's strange behavior demanded immediate solution. He alone, of the Gotham Hounds, had no alibi!

Wentworth thrust open the door of the theatre, and from the darkness close at hand, he caught the muffled cry of a woman! He found himself staring into the white, terror-strained face of a girl usher. One fist was ground distortingly into her mouth to strangle her scream. Through a long moment, she stared at Wentworth and then she turned and fled frantically into the darkness!

Incredulously, Wentworth watched her go. There was no one else near, nothing that he could see to frighten the girl. He himself had only sauntered through the door. And yet, that girl had been half-mad with terror!

With cautious haste, Wentworth gazed into the dimness of the theatre. On the brightly lighted stage Charles Maurice, one of the world's great tragedians, was gesturing his way through *Hamlet.* Among the audience, there was no stirring at all; not even the muffled sound of a cough. Surely, a great tribute to Maurice! But was it?

Suddenly, uncontrollably, Wentworth glanced over his shoulder at the darkness behind him. Nothing… nobody there, but an oath sprang harshly, unbidden, to Wentworth's lips.

The brass doorknob gave off a pale, green glow!

On the instant, Wentworth was racing on silent feet across

the rear of the theatre, speeding soundlessly down a side-aisle toward a door that would open backstage. At the drugstore, at Nita's home, brass-work had glowed like that. And uncontrollable laughter had gripped all who came near. Here, there was that same green light. But here, as the face of that usher had testified all too clearly, there was not laughter—but terror, scarcely held under control!

He knew past all doubt what held the audience spellbound. Not a great actor... but fear! Fear begotten in the same inexplicable, hellish way as that mad laughter. That terror was too horribly obvious in the stillness that gripped the audience. On the stage the actors faltered through their lines, were halting in what must have been a smoothly drilled play! Terror, or laughter, and that pale green glow... They could mean but one deadly thing.

Munro!—who planned some fresh devil's business in this theatre!

Wentworth could not guess the nature of Munro's plot. He could not understand Munro's purpose in terrorizing an entire audience. How could the man gain revenue this way? There must be some ulterior motive of gigantic scope! Possibly... no time now to ponder. Already he could feel the mounting tension of the audience like static electricity before a hurricane. He could feel its echo in himself, despite his foreknowledge, despite the power of his great will. The slightest untoward sound, the shock of a shot, and this cultured, civilized audience would become a stampede of fear-crazed animals, slaughtering each other to escape from... nothing!

SLAVES OF THE LAUGHING DEATH

A shot? Hunter had entered the theatre with a pistol; had entered and disappeared!

AS CAUTIOUSLY as if he walked among sleeping dragons, Wentworth eased up to the backstage door. His plans were still unformed, but he knew that if this breeding terror were to be controlled, it must be from the stage. And those upon whom that task would normally devolve were equally besotted with fear!

Wentworth passed through the door and it seemed to him that fluttering wings of terror beat within his own breast—in the breast of the Spider who had never known fear! He stood stock-still and his face paled with the effort at control. It took all his mighty will to steel himself to the task ahead. He knew the method he must follow.

The Spider must tread the boards!

Wentworth's movements were deliberate as he resisted every impulse to be terror-stricken. A velvet drape, snatched from a box, furnished a long cape that swung about his heels. With stiff fingers, he fashioned his black hat into a slouch that pulled low over his brows. His shoulders hunched until, in the shadows, he became a menacing and sinister figure. The audience would recognize it instantly, and the sight would spread a fresh terror... but a *known* terror.

It was the only means he could contrive. Only one thing could govern now the mob that the audience had become. One thing—a greater, counteracting fear!

Wentworth's hands crossed on his breast and when they reappeared, they balanced twin automatics. His lips twisted thinly. Laird and Warring were following him closely. They would

"Keep your seats!" he cried. "I'll kill the first man who moves!"

appear in time to see his parade in the robes of the Spider! Sardonic laughter pushed at Wentworth's throat… The Spider moved deliberately toward the wings!

At that moment, a woman screamed!

Bounding into the wings of the stage, Wentworth sent his piercing gaze among the actors, seeking the cause of that cry. It was no part of the play. The girl who played Ophelia screamed again. She covered her face with her hands and whirled toward the wings, her draperies flying. Charles Maurice stood like a man knocked out on his feet. His face was uplifted, and its expression was dazed, incredulous. Across his forehead there was a faint trace of blood. Then slowly, before Wentworth's eyes, Maurice's face took on a strange and ghastly hue.

It began to glow with small green flames!

A hoarse cry rose in the throat of the actor. He lifted his hands and his clawed fingers tore across his cheeks, and where they had dragged… the flesh came away like rotted cloth! Charles Maurice screamed then, terribly, and it was echoed by a hundred terror-laden screams from the audience.

With a long, fierce bound, Wentworth leaped upon the stage. The cape of the Spider swirled and whipped from his shoulders, and the massive guns in his fists caught sharp gleams of light. He leveled them at the audience, and his voice rang out with cold menace.

"Keep your seats!" he cried. "I'll kill the first man who moves!"

His eyes ranged the audience fiercely; saw the fear-stricken faces. But he had calculated correctly. Before this known menace, and under the threat of those leveled guns, the spectators froze in their places—all except one man!

Wentworth's gaze whipped to him, while the screams of the tortured actor rang out in his ears. He saw that one man streaking toward the rear of the balcony, and grim incredulity shook him. The man fleeing up the central aisle of the balcony was... the druggist whom Munro had killed!

There was that instant of shock, and then Wentworth's ready gun swung upward. Not the druggist, but Munro himself! Munro had loosed his horror-working chemical upon Maurice, and now was making his get-away!

Laughter surged to Wentworth's lips, and it was thin and metallic, the mocking flat laughter of the Spider! He leveled one automatic deliberately.

"You're finished, Munro!" he called.

MUNRO DID two things with incredible speed. He wrenched a woman from her aisle seat, whipping her body across his own as a shield. In the same instant, a gun flashed in his hand, its thunder echoing into the theatre vault. A brilliant flash of blue-white light flared from behind the audience... a flashlight for a picture, a picture of Wentworth in the Spider's robes!

Those two things snapped Wentworth's control over the audience. People surged to their feet. Seats splintered and crashed in the first panic of the stampede. Before the flare of the flashlight had died, the entire audience was streaming toward the doors! The screams of women, the hoarse, unhuman shouts of men drowned out every other sound. Wentworth saw a man crash his fist into a woman's face and step on her to escape. He saw a small man jerked bodily from the aisle and flung like a broken dummy over among the splintering seats. The doors were already jammed with men who struggled madly to escape from their terror, and carried their terror with them in their own breasts.

In the balcony, Munro had disappeared in the swirl of scrambling, racing human beings!

For one instant, Wentworth poised there rigidly, shouting in his effort to regain control. He sent a bullet flying over the heads of the people, and it lent only speed to their flight. He whirled and plunged into the wings. Stagehands were fighting to crowd out of a narrow exit door and Wentworth was among them in an instant. His hard fists stung the men to fury, beat them into resistance. When they looked into his white, furious face, their terror seized them anew and they tried to flee. He seized two of them by the shoulders, pinned them back against the wall, and his will blazed at them from his eyes—the will of the Spider, who was justly called the Master of Men!

"Fools!" he shouted at them. "There is nothing there to harm you! Nothing… but there is death in my hands! Get that hose! Turn it on! Drench the audience with it! Batter sense into their fool heads! Understand me? Good! The hose…."

Under the lash of his command, the men moved stumblingly to obey him. They ran out upon the stage with the hose already struggling under water pressure like a great serpent. The white stream lashed out into the audience, tumbled men helpless to the floor, beating them from their mad slaughter of their fellows. Across the stage, Wentworth bounded again and caught two of the actors. Once more the fierce drive of the Spider's will did its work and they leaped to drag down another hose and unleash it upon the audience.

Wentworth waited for no more. They would stay at the task he had set them, in very fear of the Spider!

Once more, he bounded upon the stage. Cape streaming from his shoulders, he stepped high upon the proscenium and launched himself out into space. His hands caught the edge of one of the boxes and he swung there a moment before he could muscle himself upward. Faintly, he heard the crack of a gun and, inches from his face, a bullet ploughed up the red velvet that wrapped the box's rail. Wentworth's lips tightened, but he did not glance toward the gunman. With a powerful swing, he had hurled himself over the railing and was plunging toward the dark aisle behind the boxes.

AS HE lunged out into view again, his eyes combed the wreckage of the balcony. There were a half-dozen motionless figures sprawled over the seats and in the aisles, knots of fighting human beings fought like wild beasts to escape. He saw a broad-shouldered man whip an axe from a casing on the wall and drive it into the back of a man ahead of him. In a single leap, Wentworth was upon the axe-wielder. His fist flashed to the man's jaw, hammered him inertly against the wall. He whipped out a gun and sent its thunder crashing in the ears of the mob.

"Quiet!" he snapped. "I'll shoot the next man who strikes a blow! Quietly, now, and you can all get out easily!"

He burned brick dust from the wall into the face of a man who cursed him, and after that there was quiet at that exit door. The crowd began to file out.

As abruptly as if he had been tripped, Wentworth plunged to the floor beside the man he had knocked out. Already the man was stirring. With swift gestures, Wentworth threw the cape about his shoulders, dragged the hat down on his head.

Terror stirred in the reviving man. He surged to his feet and, unmindful of cape and hat, began to flee up the aisle. Wentworth surged to his feet, brandishing the axe, and pursued him with hoarse shouts.

"Stop him!" he shouted. "Stop the Spider!"

Grimly, he followed the man fleeing in the Spider's robes. He hoped that the man would escape lead from whoever was sniping at the Spider, but if he fell he had richly deserved death for that brutal axe work! He saw the man crash into the mob at the next door, and his momentum drove him through to the metal fire escape outside. The mob, separated by his charge, became more quiet; ceased its battling and scurried through to safety.

Wentworth peered around. The balcony was almost emptied, but suddenly, high up in the rearmost seats, he caught sight of a gray-headed man who sat quietly waiting for the panic to subside. As Wentworth spotted the man, he caught the flash of a gun in his fist, and dived to the floor just in time. And exultation burned in Wentworth's throat!

That man was Munro!

Wentworth whipped out a gun, lifted himself cautiously, and was just in time to see the man pop out of a window! Wentworth whipped out a gun, lifted glass crashed there… too late! With a shout, he hurled himself through the wreckage. He took two rows of seats at a high hurdle, stumbled into the central aisle and went up the steps three at a time. Ahead of him, and to the right, he saw Carl Laird pop out of an entrance.

"Munro!" Wentworth shouted. "He went out that window!"

Laird nodded and raced up the central aisle ahead of Wentworth, but in a half dozen strides, Wentworth passed him and reached the window first. He gazed down the sheer front of the building. No retreat there for Munro. He peered upward, and saw a man's legs disappear over the edge of the roof.

Laird was beside Wentworth, and his voice came coldly. "You got rid of your Spider robes pretty quickly, Wentworth. Or am I mistaken?"

Wentworth said harshly, "If you're tracking the Spider, he went out of that side exit over there. Personally, I think he did good work, stopped a worse casualty toll. I'm chasing Munro!"

Wentworth scrambled out of the window, set his hands in the narrow ledges formed by offset in the masonry that formed steps upward to the roof. If Munro peered over the edge now, a single shot would finish off the Spider forever! He was conscious that Laird was no longer beside him; he had gone to confirm Wentworth's story of the Spider's escape, beyond a doubt! Wentworth's lips twisted bitterly. The police were like that, too; forgetting the pursuit of the real criminal in a frantic pursuit of the man who was their greatest ally against crime!

WENTWORTH CLIMBED swiftly toward the roof. His hands were too busy for guns. His toes clung to the narrow ledges. Death might wait for him there on the roof, but equally he might destroy Munro! The man had just begun his operations, and already he had spread death and horror among scores of helpless human beings. In such a chase, the Spider would never falter!

The crash of a gunshot in the street whipped Wentworth's head about. He saw Laird poised on top a taxi to which he had leaped and, almost at the corner, was the becapped figure of the axe-murderer! As Wentworth peered down, Laird fired again. The man in the Spider's cape staggered... and disappeared around the corner. In an instant, Laird was racing after him.

Wentworth swore under his breath. There could be no mercy in his heart for the man who had committed that brutal axe-murder in the theatre, but it went against the grain that he should be hunted down in the Spider's robes. No time for that now. He must climb on, capture Munro. Wentworth strained his arms outward and caught hold of the projecting roof ledge of the theatre, instantly let his body swing out into space. He hooked a knee over the verge, bellied the ledge... and a gun licked its powder flame at him from the roof balustrade!

Wentworth felt the bullet's wind brush past his ear. With a violent exertion of all the power of his mighty muscles, he heaved himself to the ledge and rolled flush against the brick balustrade. His gun was in his fist, his breath dry and brassy in his throat. For that single instant, he checked there. Then he drew his feet under him; his left hand crept to the balustrade. With an explosion of thigh muscles, he hurdled the brick rampart!

He had a glimpse of a white face, the glint of a gun, then his hurtling body crashed into that of the other man beyond the balustrade and they plunged together to the roof! The unexpected violence of the collision wrenched Wentworth's gun from his fist, sent it skittering across the graveled surface of the roof. With an acrobat's skill, Wentworth turned in the air, landed on hands and feet asprawl the body of the gunman!

Fierce and exultant laughter pumped into Wentworth's throat. There was no pause in the fierceness of his attack. His right hand clamped upon the man's throat, his left caught him by the thigh. A heave of his shoulders, and Wentworth lifted the man up out of the shadows of the roof, poised him high above the balustrade and sixty feet of empty space to the street below!

"Munro!" Wentworth panted. "Munro, this time, there will be no mistake! You die!"

He prepared to heave the man into space!

"No, no, Wentworth!" the man panted weakly. "In heaven's name, no! I didn't know it was you! I thought it was Munro!"

Wentworth stared up then at the man he held on the brink of death, and a startled oath squeezed out of his throat.

He was gazing into the terror-stricken face of... *Robert Hunter!*

CHAPTER 4
DEATH TRAP

RESTORED TO his footing on the roof, Hunter leaned weakly against the balustrade and mopped his forehead. His professional smile was sickly and forced.

"That was close," he said hoarsely. "Pretty close!"

Wentworth studied him silently. There was nothing in the

man's build to contradict Wentworth's suspicions that he might be Munro; that he had, in the garb of the druggist, hurled death upon the actor on the stage. And he was positive he had seen Munro flee to this roof only moments before himself.

His eyes turned from Hunter and swept the roof carefully. He had not exonerated Hunter, but the Spider could not execute his justice upon a man whom he merely suspected. Yet the roof offered no hiding place. There was a slit of light from a stair kiosk door that swung half open, but aside from that entrance the roof offered no escape—none save another wall such as Wentworth had climbed.

"You came up the stairs?" he asked harshly.

Hunter nodded eagerly. "I was leaning out a window and saw the druggist start his climb up here. I rushed up the stairs, but the mob delayed me some. When I saw you swing over the edge, I thought you were the druggist who killed the actor, and I blazed away. God, that was close!"

"I don't know yet," Wentworth said softly, "just how you happened to come here… or why you knocked down the policeman and stole his gun!"

Hunter laughed, waved a hand airily. The hand didn't tremble much. His stance was heroic, legs braced, head lifted challengingly—a pose in which he had been photographed before the Taj Mahal; beside the Dalai Lama of Tibet.

"Oh, that!" Hunter chuckled. "I needed a gun, that was all. As soon as I heard that dying man's story in your apartment, I knew that something must be wrong in the drug store. I darted over and kept watch. After you went in, and there was shooting,

I saw this man in a druggist's white coat duck out of a basement window and so I followed him. He changed his coat in a car, and then came into this theatre. I thought I would need a gun to challenge him, and so I... borrowed one!"

Wentworth said quietly, "Do you think you could point out the druggist's car from up here?"

Hunter shook his head, "I'm afraid not. You see, it was chauffeur-driven, and went on after the man got out. I'm afraid I didn't notice the license number either. Damned careless of me. But you see, in the places where I usually go, they don't have cars or license numbers. This detective business is new to me."

Wentworth said without emphasis, "Quite so. I think I'd like to have a look at the dead man on the stage. Poor Maurice."

He gestured Hunter toward the kiosk door, and Hunter walked before him with a deliberate swagger. "You're suspicious of me," he said, with a show of frankness, "and I can't say I blame you. But you're dead wrong, Wentworth. Dead wrong."

An uncanny silence lay over the theatre into which they descended. A woman lifted herself heavily from the aisle into which she had fallen and walked with the slow, steady movements of an automaton past them toward the exit doors. Her left arm hung limply, broken. The brilliant stage lighting still blazed down upon the fallen body of Charles Maurice, glinted on the whiteness of his fleshless skull. Into that silence, as Wentworth descended the last flight of stairs, lifted the burred voice of Carl Laird.

"Confound it, man, I don't care about your orders!" he was

saying forcefully. "I tell you I pursued the Spider out of this theatre. He got away, and I have to rejoin my friends inside!"

Hunter started toward the door, told the policeman pompously, "It's quite all right, my man. Mr. Laird is known to me!" **BEHIND WENTWORTH**, the two men walked toward the stage. The forced gaiety of Hunter's tones, repeating the story of his pursuit of the druggist, his encounter with Wentworth on the roof, was hollow in the dim auditorium. A fierce urgency was working in Wentworth's breast. He had to decide about Hunter. If the man were guilty, he must not be allowed to continue this work of slaughter and terrorization. At the same time, if he were guilty, Nita was safe so long as Wentworth kept Hunter under surveillance. If he were innocent....

Wentworth smothered a sharp oath as he stepped back stage. Ralph Warring's sprawled body lay just inside the door. He held a flashbulb gun in his fist, but the straps of his camera had been sliced, and the camera was gone! Under Wentworth's ministrations, Warring recovered. He surged to his feet, fists striking out fiercely.

"The Spider!" he said hoarsely. "Damn it, the Spider stole my camera!"

Laird thrust forward. "When?" he demanded harshly.

Warring rubbed his forehead with a heavy hand. "How the hell do I know?" he demanded irritably. "He jumped at me out of the shadows when I came backstage. I saw his cape swirling, got a glimpse of his face under the hat-brim. That was all."

"How long was that after you snapped a picture of the Spider in the balcony?" Wentworth asked quietly.

Warring shook his head, then snapped his fingers. "I remember now!" he said. "I saw you chasing the Spider with an axe in your hand! The Spider got out the door, and I ran back here, thinking I could get a shot of the whole theatre from the stage. He must have run down the fire escape, doubled back and... hell, I don't see how he could. It was too fast! But he did it; I swear I saw him!"

Wentworth frowned at Warring, turned sharply toward the stage. Munro could not be the one who had snatched the camera, since Munro had been at that moment climbing through a window, or scrambling up the face of the building. Hunter, by his own story, was leaning out of another window at that moment. Laird had been beside Wentworth... Wentworth's lips tightened. Only one explanation was possible. Ralph Warring was lying! But, in the name of heaven, why?

Wentworth stood staring down at the pitiful corpse of one of the world's great actors. He stooped slowly and picked up the sword that lay beside Maurice's hand. It was a keen blade, scarcely the regulation stage sword, and Maurice had ripped it out at the last minute when he was attacked.

From the darkness at the theatre's back, a man called sharply, "All of you stand just like that! Don't move!"

Wentworth caught the glitter of police brass in the dimness, heard the heavy clump of feet as several men moved down the aisle toward him. Abruptly, Wentworth's eyes narrowed. By the heavens, Munro had overstepped himself this time! Maurice's death would end by trapping him! And Nita… Nita was in fearful and imminent danger!

Wentworth whirled, and the challenge of the police came to him again. He caught the glint of a leveled gun! Laird and Warring were moving toward him across the width of the stage.

"It's quite all right, officer," Wentworth said quietly. "We have no need to escape."

He flipped the sword into the air, caught it by the tip of the blade and held it swaying for a moment. He laughed and sent it flashing off into the darkness of the wings. He saw Laird glance at him sharply as he moved forward to the lip of the stage. Warring moved forward with Laird, but Wentworth hung back a pace. He flung a sharp glance upward at the heavy asbestos curtain just behind the proscenium arch and slid a sidelong look off into the shadows. Yes, the sword had flown true. The rope that held the asbestos curtain had been sliced almost through, was rapidly unraveling….

Wentworth began to talk rapidly. "That audience was deliberately stampeded to distract attention from the murder of Maurice," he said. "He was killed by a fragile glass bomb thrown into his face from the balcony. The bomb contained a corrosive gas that, as you see, ate away the flesh from his face!"

A cop swore harshly. "Don't give me that stuff!" he said. "I supposed a bomb full of gas robbed the theatre safe, too!"

"A blind, purely a blind!" Wentworth said rapidly. "You see, by killing Maurice, the murderer gave me a valuable clue. Now, I know how to find... *Munro!*" And he knew something else, too. He knew Munro's purpose in this pointless seeming slaughter!

WARRING AND Laird were staring at Wentworth. Hunter, strolling out of the wings, laughed loudly. "I told you we would do well to invite Wentworth to join the Gotham Hounds!" he cried.

It was at that moment the asbestos curtain's halyard snapped. Its sound was not loud, but the sudden downward rush of the curtain itself had the mounting whisper of a descending avalanche! Hunter cried out hoarsely, leaped out of its path, and the weighted bottom struck the stage just behind him. Wentworth was instantly alone, shut off from the theatre and all the others by the swift drop of the curtain.

On the instant, Wentworth had caught up the inert body of the dead actor and thrown it across his shoulder. With long bounds, he crossed the stage and reached the exit door on the narrow dark alley which ran beside the theatre. Behind him, he heard the crazy shouting of the police, the crash of a discharged gun, but he did not check his race. They were still trying to get backstage, and he had, perhaps, a minute's start.

Ahead of him, a uniformed man sprang into the mouth of the alley, fumbled out his gun.

"Don't shoot, officer!" Wentworth cried. "I've got an injured man here! Quick, a car! An ambulance!"

He made his voice loud, and the alley funneled it ahead, sent it booming out into the street. As he blundered past the hesitant policeman, his Daimler rolled forward easily, and Jackson, ever alert for the slightest signal, leaped out to fling wide the door.

"You can use this car, sir!" Jackson cried. "What hospital?"

Wentworth leaped into the back, tossed Maurice's body to the cushions. "Roosevelt is near," he snapped, and turned toward the still uncertain policeman. "Tell them where I've gone," he said, and slammed the door.

Instantly, the car was racing down toward Broadway. The swirling crowd parted before the insistent demand of the horn, and Wentworth leaned forward to hurl swift instructions at Jackson.

"To Miss Nita's!" he said, with cold violence, "and let nothing delay you. Her life is in deadly peril!"

The hum of the motor deepened. Jackson's hands, bulging from their grip on the wheel, handled the heavy car like a toy. Traffic parted desperately at the urgency of the horn.

"As soon as we reach there," Wentworth said rapidly, "you will cut back to my house. Put this body under refrigeration at once. If police are there, you will have to circumvent them."

Jackson's voice came back in bursts because of his concentration on driving. "They know you got him, sir!"

"I'll see Kirkpatrick meantime!" Wentworth snapped. "Get on with your driving, man; we're barely crawling!"

The speedometer needle wavered up another ten miles to sixty. It would have been suicide, or murder, for any other driver than Jackson. Wentworth bent grimly over the ghastly body, set deliberately about fingerprinting it with equipment which he carried always in the car. Afterward, with a magnifying glass, he set about extracting their index.

"P—thirteen—nineteen—O, over twenty-three—seventeen—nineteen—twelve," he murmured.

Rapidly, he committed the index to memory. Wentworth had long ago learned that written records were less reliable than his memory. They might fall into the wrong hands. When he had finished his task, the Daimler was sliding to a halt before Riverside Towers, where Nita van Sloan lived. Wentworth sprang to the pavement, and instantly the Daimler was underway again.

THE DOZEN steps necessary to enter the building and reach the elevator required an endless time, and the sighing motion of the cage seemed laborious. Yet it was less than a dozen seconds before he was striding down the deep carpeted corridor of the twenty-first floor toward Nita's apartment. Hope and fear contested within him like warring armies, and it was fear that won when finally he rounded the angle of the corridor and could see Nita's door. An oath of despair lifted like a sob into his throat, and he hurled himself into a furious sprint over those last few yards.

In the dimness of the corridor, the brass knob of Nita's door glimmered with a pale and evil greenish light!

Wentworth wasted no time on the formality of ringing the bell. From a vertical pocket inside his vest, he slipped out a slim tool of surgical steel. It clashed against the lock and, seconds later, the door gave under his hand. He bounded through… and in the recesses of the apartment, Nita screamed!

The cry was high and tearing, mad with terror, and Went-

He rounded through the living room, brought up against the locked door of her boudoir. He leaned against it tensely, listening. Through the thin panels, he could hear her breathing, shallow and hurried with fear… and she would not answer.

"Nita, dear," he whispered softly. "Please open the door. It's Dick! Please, I want to help you!"

She did not answer, and Wentworth dropped to his knee, peered through the keyhole. At first, there was only darkness and then he saw the shifting lights on Nita's dress. She was moving backward. Her white, tense hands were thrust out toward the door, and horror twisted all the sweet lines of her face. Half across the room, she checked. She twisted her head about and stared behind her… *toward the open window!*

A shout lifted to Wentworth's lips and died there. He could see electric tension run through Nita, could see a mad hope light her face. She turned and began to creep toward the window. And that window opened onto nothingness. Below it were twenty-one stories of empty space!

Frantically, Wentworth whipped out his lockpick again, and set it in the lock. He must operate without any sound at all, lest he hurry Nita's approach to death! The lock was stubborn, and Wentworth saw that, for once, his hands were trembling. He brushed an arm across his forehead, forced himself to steadiness. And all the while, the cold fear that had no origin in fact, but could drive men mad with fear, gnawed like a saw-toothed rat at his heart. What was happening beyond this door? He could not withdraw the pick to look again, and seconds were flying. Seconds… and it would take so pitifully few to destroy Nita!

At last the stubborn lock yielded. Instantly, Wentworth flung the door wide and leaped across the room. A shout of horror burned his throat. Nita was poised on the window sill, peering down into darkness with a fearful fascination upon her face. She took the time to cast one more look back at Wentworth, and in that split-second instant, Wentworth caught her about the waist. He snatched her from the brink of death.

BEFORE HER feet struck the floor, Nita was fighting him. She was beating at him with her small white fists, drumming at him with her resolute heels. All Wentworth's pleading went unheeded. It required all his strength to wrestle her back from the gaping invitation of the window, toward which his own eyes swung with a fascinated fear.

It was while he stared, while he struggled with Nita, that he caught sight of something that flashed briefly in the outpouring light of the room; something that was hurtling forward out of the black obscurity of the night! Wentworth caught a single glimpse of the thing as it darted into the room, a glittering sphere in which something green and amorphous and horrible writhed like a living thing!

"Munro's bomb!" Wentworth gasped.

He speared a hand toward the fragile sphere, and the wrench of Nita's unremitting struggle kept him from reaching it! The bomb sailed on across the room and smashed against the wall! Instantly, pale green tendrils were lifting into the air, reaching toward them! Wentworth swung Nita clear of the floor, started forward in a dash from the room—and another of the spheres flashed overhead to spatter its tinkling fragments on the wall!

A pattern of horror in green was spider-webbed across the only exit!

With a choked curse, Wentworth wheeled back from the door. Only one exit remaining and that was the one which Nita had fought to use… a window twenty-one stories above the street!

Wentworth reached the wall beside the window, he drew Nita toward him, and forced her wide-staring eyes to focus upon his. He stooped to her lips… Through a long moment more, Nita fought him furiously with the madness that Munro had sent. Gradually, she quieted. She answered the kiss of the man she loved.

"Dick!" she whispered. "Oh, Dick, it's really you! I've gone almost mad. First, everything seemed so wonderful, so gay, and then suddenly, I was terrified."

"Later, dear, I'll tell you everything," Wentworth told her softly. "We have work to do. Munro is trying to kill us!"

"Munro!" Nita shuddered. She peered about the familiar safety of her room, and drew closer to Wentworth. "That gas!" she whispered. "I understand now, who made that green gas!"

"Yes. It destroys human flesh," Wentworth said shortly. "We have to escape by the window. Munro will undoubtedly try to stop us, Nita." He snatched up a jar from Nita's dressing table and smashed the ceiling light. Darkness fell softly upon the room, but through the dark those green tendrils could creep, tendrils of death. Wentworth peered cautiously out the window. There was a narrow ledge, and the steel casements of the windows swung outward. Far below were the streaming lanes of Riverside Drive traffic, the black gleaming breast of the Hudson River. The sweet breath of the spring night drifted in. Wentworth fought down a shudder.

"Munro is above us," Wentworth said quietly. "He is in this same building!"

NITA WAS close beside him, and he began to unwind from about his waist a length of silken cord which the police knew as the Spider's Web.

"In what disguise is Munro this time?" Nita asked. "I have my gun in my hand."

"I haven't seen him," Wentworth said quietly, as he knotted the silken cord beneath Nita's arms. "But he threw bombs in through this window. The only way that could be managed would be for Munro to whip them down from above with a length of cord... Here, Nita!"

They balanced there on the brink of death, and Wentworth peered cautiously upward along the sheer face of the building. He steadied himself against the out-swung casement, and coiled the silken line in his hand. Directly overhead, another casement window swung open, but Wentworth ignored that. If Munro were inside, waiting, even the Spider would stand no chance at all!

"I'll get a loop over the next window above and to the left," Wentworth whispered. "Our best chance is to get out through the apartment next to yours, and take Munro from behind!"

Wentworth's movements were swift despite his deliberation,

and presently he had thrown a loop over the steel-framed, open window he had chosen: one floor up, second row over.

"Keep your gun ready," Wentworth whispered. "If all is clear, I'll toss the web back to you, then you swing over to me!"

Deftly, he twisted the silken line about his arm, and with no further delay, swung off into space. His gaze was concentrated fiercely on the narrow sill where he must catch and hold until he could maneuver around the steel casement which stood open. Below him was two hundred feet and more of empty space. Men moved like ants on the pavement far below. But he could not think of  them; dared not! Behind him, Nita screamed a warning, and her gun blasted punctuation to her scream!

"Munro!" she cried. "Above you, Dick! *Munro!*"

Wentworth kept his eyes on the narrow sill where he must balance, heard the gun slam out again, again. Fragments of glass rained down before him, catching tiny silver glints of light from the open casement. Wentworth strangled an oath. That glass could have but one meaning. Instead of being in the apartment directly over Nita's, Munro was lying in wait for him behind the window to which his rope was attached!

Even as the thought slashed across Wentworth's mind, he felt a shock in the strand to which he clung, and knew that something—probably a sharp blade—must have struck it. Nita's gun yammered hysterically behind him. Wentworth lifted his left leg high and reached out before him. If only he could get his knee hooked over that casement!

The rope slipped a fraction of an inch….

In the same instant, Wentworth realized that he was too low to get a leg over the casement. Frenziedly, he flung himself forward. It was the only chance. He released his hold on the silken rope and dived for the casement with both reaching hands!

As he plunged through the air, he saw the line of the silken rope writhing loosely before his face, severed by Munro! The next instant, Wentworth's hands clamped down on the top of the casement. His body swung violently forward, and the steel frame caught him across the belly, drove the wind from his lungs. Then Wentworth transferred the grip of his right hand to the inner edge of the casement, and hooked his other arm over the window sill. He accomplished that to the timing of Nita's gun, and even as his bent arm clamped home against the inner wall, he realized that she had emptied her gun! Until she took the time to reload, there was no threat to keep Munro from striking him down!

CLINGING THERE to the face of the wall, body and legs dangling in space, Wentworth did an incredible thing. He freed one hand and wrenched out his gun and for the first time peered upward toward his ancient and terrible enemy!

Even as he stared, Munro was leaning out of the window. His head was encased in a huge metal helmet such as shallow-water divers use. Through the vision panel, his eyes glittered hostilely.

His right hand was raised high above his head, and in that fist shimmered a greenish sphere—a gas bomb!

In the same instant that the man's hand swept downward, Wentworth fired. Munro's helmeted head was driven upward and back. The gas bomb arched outward into the night, spun past within inches of Wentworth's upturned face… and Munro was no longer at the window. For an instant, his left hand gripped the casement there, but even as Wentworth loosed another bullet, the hand was jerked from sight. It seemed to Wentworth he heard a muffled curse, but he could not be sure.

Had he killed Munro? No time to speculate on that. He had to get into the apartment from whose window he swung, get to Munro's hideout. His left arm ached intolerably. It had been badly wrenched in that first violent swing against the window and, for long minutes now, it had supported his entire weight. Only the exertion of his powerful will compelled that arm to function.

Wentworth did not wait to holster his gun. He tossed it in through the window, clamped his right arm also over the window sill and heaved himself upward… It was only then that he peered into the room beyond the casement. He swore incredulously, and checked his effort to drag himself inside. It was a woman's boudoir into which he looked. The woman was here, but she had been utterly silent throughout the whole battle.

The woman was seated before a dressing table, and there was a powder-puff in her hand… but the face that stared back from the mirrors had no eyes at all; nor any flesh. It was a skull only.

Wentworth's weakened arms almost lost their hold… and

the realization dinned in upon his brain that he dared not enter this room! For here, the devouring gas of Munro lurked. In the apartment above, Munro himself was waiting. He clung, and turned his white face slowly toward Nita. For an instant, he stared blankly at the empty sill to which Nita had clung. Fear surged through him, then he heard her call.

"Here, Dick!" she cried. "I'm at the window below! I've fastened the web to my window for safety, but when I throw you the other end, tie it and slide down here!"

It was an incredible time that elapsed before Nita's third throw brought the silken line up to Wentworth. An eternity before his fatigued hands could arrange the loop as he wanted it. Then he slid down through the air, and but for the strong grip of Nita's arm, would have plunged on to his death.

The instant she had guided him through the window, he was running across the room. He heard the rapid tattoo of Nita's heels behind him as he wrenched open the door, sped along the hallway of this unfamiliar apartment. Munro... Munro was two stories above, and Wentworth still had a gun!

HE WAS sprinting when he reached the hallway, his feet soundless on the deep carpets. At the stairs, he flung back words to Nita.

"Hide behind this radiator. Reload your gun!" he said, but softly. "If he gets past me, and starts down... shoot! And don't stop shooting until your gun is empty!"

Nita dropped back as Wentworth spoke, and her eyes were wide and dark with apprehension. Not for herself, but for Dick, racing so valiantly into a battle while he still reeled from the fatigue of that struggle with death on the building's sheer side. She crouched behind the steam radiator, jacked a cartridge from the fresh clip into the chamber, and thumbed off the safety. Her hand was tense, but very steady. After a while, her forearm began to ache....

Wentworth burst out of the stairway well, and heard the door of the elevator open. A man in operator's uniform looked out, blinked stupidly at Wentworth.

"You ring, sir?" he asked.

Wentworth snapped, "Lock that control lever in place! Come with me!"

He had no gun in his hand, but the accent of command was in his voice. The man stared at him open-mouthed, but his hands were already moving to obey. He set the catch which held the door open, and moved awkwardly out into the hallway. Wentworth caught his arm and thrust him along the corridor as he hurried toward the entrance of Munro's hideout. The door swung open. The apartment was empty!

Wentworth swore under his breath and his eyes combed the open windows, the wreckage of glass that Nita's bullets had wrought. There was no sign of Munro. The helmet, then, had been bullet-proof although Wentworth had flung his lead against the vision window. He knew that it had sped true, for the shock had driven Munro back inside the window.

"All right," Wentworth said quietly. "We'll go down now."

Disappointment weighed heavily upon him. During those few swift moments while he had slid down the web to Nita, Munro had made good his escape... He stopped the elevator two floors down and called to Nita, who came rapidly to meet him. The operator's head swung toward Nita. His eyes were admiring beneath the frosty sheen of white brows.

"He got away!" Nita said somberly.

Wentworth smiled slightly as the elevator sighed downward. "A master of disguise like Munro, needs only a few minutes to disappear," he said. "I noticed that the police have been summoned. They undoubtedly have the building surrounded, and a close search will reveal whether there are any disguised persons in the building. Operator, I wish you'd come with me. You should know everyone in the building well enough to tell whether they're disguised."

The operator said, "Disguised?" He stopped the cage and slid open the door at the first floor. Three men were surging in through the main door, and Wentworth smiled grimly as he recognized them; saw a fourth man striding energetically forward behind them.

The Gotham Hounds had arrived, and brought Stanley Kirkpatrick, the commissioner of police, with them!

"Come along!" Wentworth said to the operator. "I'm sure you can penetrate any disguise we encounter."

Hunter flashed his wide, toothy smile. "We've got a clue to Munro!" he cried. "The Gotham Hounds will get him yet!"

Wentworth was still smiling, "An expert in disguises, such as you," he was saying to the elevator operator. "You did an excellent job, really, but you forgot that when bullet-proof glass is fractured, such as the glass in Munro's helmet, it throws off a fine powder of glass... such as is caught in your eyebrows!

"Gentlemen!" Wentworth clamped a hand hard on the nape of the elevator operator's neck, jammed a gun into his side. "Gentlemen, allow me to present... *Munro!*"

CHAPTER 5
CELL FOR THE SPIDER!

B LANK INCREDULITY stared at Wentworth out of the faces of the four men who confronted him; and none of them seemed more stupid, more lacking in understanding, than the elevator operator whom Wentworth gripped by the neck. Nita had drawn her automatic as he spoke, leveled it at the man in the uniform of an apartment attendant. She backed away two yards, as Wentworth had taught her. When two captors were so separated, it was hard for a prisoner to shake both of them....

Kirkpatrick took a stiff stand before Wentworth, his carriage erect as a soldier, the spiked ends of his waxed mustache bristling. "Dick," he said coldly, "if this is some trickery, I warn you that you won't succeed in diverting my attention! You're going to pay for kidnapping that body from the theatre!"

Wentworth nodded, but did not glance toward his friend. He respected Kirkpatrick, and knew that this was no petty irritation that the commissioner expressed. Wentworth had violated a law; and all law was sacred to Stanley Kirkpatrick! Wentworth was looking at his captive with painful intensity, watching for any hostile move. The man made none. He cringed under Wentworth's grip.

"Aw, what's the matter with you, mister?" he whined. "I ain't done nothing."

"Only four murders within the last two hours," Wentworth said softly. "Plus God knows how many deaths at the theatre, and we won't even speak of your attempt to kill Miss van Sloan and myself!... No, Kirkpatrick, this is no advertisement. I call your attention to the fact that, though this man apparently is an elevator operator, there are no calluses on his hand from throwing the lever. In fact, there is on his left hand, a smear of green paint... put there by my bullet which just missed his hand as he gripped the steel frame of a casement window."

The operator writhed under Wentworth's grip. "You're nuts!" he said. "I'm a substitute, and I got that paint fixing a window for a lady on the twenty-first floor! I can prove it if you give me a chance."

Wentworth laughed shortly. "You're always a quick thinker, Munro. You'll say, no doubt, that it was in the apartment where now a woman is dead! Is that right?"

His prisoner lifted an appealing hand to Kirkpatrick. "Look, mister, you're a cop I guess, from what you said. This guy ain't got no right to treat me like this. I ain't done nothing!"

Kirkpatrick's eyes shifted uncertainly from Wentworth to his prisoner. "There is powdered glass in your eyebrows," he said slowly. "Have you an explanation for that?"

The man started to speak, but Wentworth cut in on him softly. "Kirk, you'll admit that whatever else may be explained, there is no reason for an elevator operator to wear... a disguise!" As he spoke, he reached out his hand with a lightning-deft movement… and clamped his thumb and forefinger on his prisoner's nose! The man yelled, wrenched away… and the tip of his nose came loose in Wentworth's grip!

"Putty!" Wentworth said, "and rather incompetently stuck on."

In the same moment, the man wrenched free of Wentworth's grip and darted toward the doors!

"My man!" Wentworth called easily.

His hand flashed to the gun he had momentarily holstered, came free and the automatic lifted in steady rhythm. Wentworth's blue-gray eyes, which could be so kindly and humane, were implacable. The smile hardened on his lips, and the gun began its downward drop. The Gotham Hounds had scattered from the charge of the prisoner; Kirkpatrick was still fumbling for his gun… and, near the door, the man with the misshapen nose whipped about his head. He saw the gun falling into line, and he read his doom in Wentworth's eyes!

He faced Wentworth and flung both his hands high.

"I quit!" he cried. "I surrender! Don't shoot, Wentworth!"

WENTWORTH'S GUN was in line at arm's length, and his eyes looked calmly along the barrel. There was regret in Wentworth's gaze.

The man, whose shoulders had been cringing, stood very stiffly. A faint smile stirred his mouth.

"You're a resolute man, Wentworth," he said. "You were going to kill me."

Wentworth said, flatly. "Of course. For four murders tonight. For a hundred in the past, Munro."

Kirkpatrick uttered a low, amazed oath. "It is Munro!" he cried. "I've heard that voice before! Wentworth—"

"Get handcuffs on Munro!" Wentworth interrupted. "He's not a man to take chances with. Handcuff him to me! I'll be responsible for him!"

Munro's voice was respectful. "I didn't know you were in command of the police, too, Wentworth!"

A slow flush touched Kirkpatrick's cheekbones. "Enough of that! *Sergeant Reams!*"

The bluff sergeant who was Kirkpatrick's aide thrust through the glass doors behind Munro. Two other uniformed men followed him.

"Reams, those two men will handcuff themselves to the prisoner," Kirkpatrick ordered sharply. "He is a dangerous murderer. I hold you personally responsible!"

"That's a mistake, Kirk," Wentworth said softly.

Kirkpatrick whirled toward Wentworth as the two policemen moved stolidly forward to obey, but Wentworth kept his eyes on Munro, and his gun also. He did not move until the two men had each handcuffed a hand to Munro, and were ushering him out of the door.

"Nice work, Wentworth!" Munro called back. "I'll have to settle with you for this! My humble regards, Miss van Sloan!"

Wentworth said softly, to Kirkpatrick, "I'm going along!"

"You're staying here!" Kirkpatrick snapped. "Where is Maurice's body?"

Wentworth shook his head. "It isn't Maurice, Kirk. It was Maurice's understudy!"

Kirkpatrick said grimly, "Then he fooled the entire cast of Hamlet, as well as the audience. Stop evading me! Where is the body? I warn you, Dick, that you're under arrest on charges of interfering with the police in the performance of their duty! Also, tampering with evidence!"

Wentworth was only half listening. His acute attention was focused on the departing police, on Munro outside the building. He said, impatiently, "All right, Kirk. I accept the charges, and I'll plead guilty. But I'm still telling you it was not Maurice, but his understudy. If you know Maurice at all, you know that he never spoke to any member of the cast outside of strict business. He made a fetish of keeping to himself. Under those circumstances, and with the understudy's help, it would be easy for the other man to imitate Maurice. Here's a way to prove it. I can give you the fingerprint index of the corpse, and you can compare them with prints in Maurice's home! How about having that checked now!"

Kirkpatrick stared at Wentworth with narrowed eyes, nodded abruptly. "All right. I've rarely known you to be wrong, Dick. Sergeant Reams... check this fingerprint index with what you can find in Maurice's home. Relay the message to headquarters!"

The Gotham Hounds had been passive auditors of most of this, but now Hunter strolled forward. In the background, Laird wore a scowl on his dour face, and Warring's slitted eyes were amused as ever. Hunter was affably smiling.

"Look here, Wentworth, you're rather messing things up with this corpse-kidnapping," he said. "We've all had ourselves sworn in as special deputies to hunt the Spider. I'm afraid the commissioner won't do the same for you, now."

Wentworth smiled. "Quite all right," he said. "I'm afraid I'd find the badge hampering to... the Spider. I rather approve of the Spider these days!"

KIRKPATRICK SAID sharply, "In just what way, Dick, would your badge hamper the Spider!"

"My dear Stanley!" Wentworth cried. "It should be perfectly obvious! When once I have given my word, I invariably keep it! So the Spider might find it inconvenient, if I swore to apprehend him!"

Kirkpatrick checked an impatient oath, but his eyes continued their narrow regard of Wentworth. Laird said, sourly, "If you're suspicious of Wentworth, I can definitely prove to you that he's the Spider."

Wentworth kept a rigid smile on his lips, but it was difficult to keep the sudden apprehension out of his eyes. He felt Nita move closer to him, knew that she had the gun in her fist. Laird's face seemed angry.

"I chased the Spider in the theatre tonight," he said shortly, "and put a bullet through his shoulder. Now, if Wentworth has my bullet in his shoulder, he's guilty. Otherwise not! And I can't see any evidence of a wound!"

"And I," said Warring gently, "took some excellent pictures of the Spider tonight. Unfortunately, someone stole my pet camera, and I haven't been able to interest the police in finding it for me!"

Hunter laughed gaily, "In fact, Kirkpatrick, we have the Spider all sewed up in a sack, just as neatly as Wentworth here sewed

DR. SABRUNSKI

LAIRD

up Munro. Signed, sealed, and delivered!" Hunter's last word checked on his lips a half-uttered sound, and his eyes glared wide in sudden fright. Every man in that lobby save Wentworth was transfixed. Perhaps, he was more used to horror. For it was pure horror that split the night apart; the scream of a man in unbearable agony!

"I warned you, Kirk!" Wentworth snapped, and bounded toward the doors, gun already in his fist.

Kirkpatrick's voice rang out sharply. "Halt, Wentworth! My gun is on you!"

Wentworth said savagely, "Damn it, Kirk. Munro—"

The screams continued incredibly, and Kirkpatrick reached Wentworth's side with two long strides. A handcuff snapped its chill steel about his wrist, but Wentworth paid it no heed. He surged eagerly forward beside his friend, the commissioner of police, and they went out on the sidewalk together. Two men, two horrors, were running toward them. They wore police uniforms, and their wrists were handcuffed together, each to the other. Their faces... were *dissolving!*

Even as Wentworth saw them, the flesh streamed from their faces and he was gazing

HUNTER

WARRING

into the blank eye sockets of two skulls set upon living men! For just that second, the two inhuman things continued to stumble forward. Then they pitched to the sidewalk, and writhed out the last agony of their lives.

Munro had vanished.

Kirkpatrick stared down at the bodies of his officers. Wentworth knew that he felt those deaths with a personal pain, for he was father as well as commander to his men; and Wentworth had warned him! But Munro could not be far away!

Wentworth wrenched at the handcuff that bound him to Kirkpatrick, urged him into a pounding run toward the corner. The sound of swift traffic hummed from Riverside Drive. A few cars had swerved in toward the curb. Wentworth reached the corner, straining at the steel links that bound him to the reeling Kirkpatrick, but the side street, too, was empty.

Abruptly, Kirkpatrick snapped from his lethargy. "My car, Dick!" he barked.

Two strides, and he was at the microphone of his two-way radio, hurling a general alarm out for Munro. Wentworth shook his head hopelessly. The description would not help at all. Just now, Munro was a mousy man in the uniform of an elevator operator, with sandy-gray hair, and cringing shoulders. Five minutes from now, he could be Kirkpatrick himself, or Wentworth… or the Mayor of the city! Once let that man get out of sight, and he was as impalpable as a handful of smoke.

WENTWORTH'S LIPS closed bitterly. He, and he alone, was to blame for Munro's escape! He had allowed himself to be merciful for one moment; he had allowed himself to be swayed by the fact that the police were all about the building. That momentary weakness had already brought death in horrid form to those two officers; it might bring death to scores of others!

Sergeant Reams ran up heavily, gun in his fist, stared down in shocked amazement at the two dead men.

"My fault, sir!" he stammered presently. "But, God, he was handcuffed! We searched him!"

"Gas ducts along the backs of his arms, I imagine," Wentworth said slowly. "A reservoir within his trouser legs, perhaps. And some sort of protective substance on his hands... I know he left no prints on the lever of the elevator for I looked to see. I should have warned you, Reams. But talk of blame is foolish. We have to start over again! Kirk, get me to headquarters! I want to arrange bail on this charge of yours and get on with the fight!"

Reams shook his head heavily. "I was forgetting, Commissioner. They say down at headquarters they picked up Jackson. He had been batted over the head, and there wasn't any corpse in the car, nor in Mr. Wentworth's apartment either."

Wentworth choked down a cry, and his lips straightened more grimly. "Will you believe me now, when I tell you it wasn't Maurice!" he said. "Let's get to headquarters!"

"Another report, sir," Reams broke in. "A screwy thing. The watchman at the Nation's Bank phoned up headquarters and asked for a special guard. It seems that when he went by the vault a while ago, he noticed the dial shining sort of funny, like it had radium paint on it. Green, you know!"

Wentworth laughed sharply. "There's luck, Kirkpatrick! Let's get to that bank fast!"

Kirkpatrick turned his head heavily. "What do you mean, Dick?"

"That green glow means… that Munro is going to rob the bank! Come on, there's no time to be lost! Damn it, Kirk, I'll explain while we're on the way!" He saw a stubborn set come over Kirkpatrick's jaw and exploded angrily. "Damn your stubborn Scot's head! A few minutes ago I asked you to let me watch Munro, and you didn't listen to me!"

Kirkpatrick's face whitened, and anger touched his brilliant blue eyes darkly, but he nodded his head slowly. "That's just—" he said thickly. "All right, Wentworth, I'll listen this time. But you are going to jail!"

Kirkpatrick began to snap out orders, commanded a patrol wagon to meet him at the Nation's Bank to take charge of Wentworth; curtly refused to allow the Gotham Hounds or Nita to accompany him.

"You professional adventurers run along and bother the Spider for a while," he said shortly. "Nita, I'm sorry, but the safest thing you can do is to go home. And I suppose, phone Dick's lawyer."

The commissioner's big limousine rolled from the curb, swung eastward and began to gather speed behind the mounting scream of its siren.

"Cut that thing off!" Kirkpatrick snapped. "Now, Dick, I want explanations, in detail. Why does a green glow on the bank vault's dial mean that Munro is going to rob it?"

Wentworth explained rapidly everything that he had found out, that he had guessed about Munro. "He has some device for generating either gaiety or fear. He may be able to build up any other sort of emotion. I don't know that, and I don't know the method. Since he uses a gas to destroy men, he may use a gas for this other. I only know that whenever this… device is operating, brass or copper or its compounds begin to glow like radium! It almost sounds as if there were some electricity or a ray employed. But I don't think Munro will strike tonight, Kirk. Such a device as he uses obviously would be more potent against a crowd than individuals. My guess would be he'll strike either at the morning rush hour, or at lunch time. Place men high up in the surrounding buildings, Kirk, but do it secretly. I believe they should be above the level of this new device of Munro's."

KIRKPATRICK STARED thoughtfully ahead. He shook his head sharply. "Damn it, there must be some way to trap this man, Munro! If only we could hit on some means of identifying him… This business at the theatre has me stopped. I don't believe the murder had any significance. Just a trick to start the stampede as a cover for robbing the safe."

Wentworth was utterly relaxed against the cushions. The handcuff chafed his wrist a little, and there was iron in his soul. The Spider must be free when Munro struck!

"You can easily prove your theory on the theatre tragedy, Kirk," he said softly.

Kirkpatrick swore softly. "It's not a theory. Just a guess. I'll admit, to you, that I'm baffled!"

"Check the fingerprints!" Wentworth said. "They will prove that it was the understudy who died. Then you need only locate Maurice and ask him a few questions."

Kirkpatrick's head turned slowly. "Why don't you say what you mean, instead of hinting, Dick?" he demanded harshly.

Wentworth lifted a shoulder in a shrug. "I'm not sure what I mean!" he said shortly. "What about those fingerprints?"

Kirkpatrick leaned forward and picked up the microphone, asked headquarters for a report on the work in Maurice's apartment.

"Report is negative, sir," the announcer said. "Can't find any prints in that apartment to match with the index you gave us. And here's a report just came in, sir. The body kidnapped from the theatre has been found, in abandoned car. Can't take fingerprints. Flesh is all gone from the hands, too!"

Kirkpatrick ripped out a harsh, strange oath. "That's torn it, Dick!" he cried. "That body was kidnapped from Jackson solely to destroy the fingerprints. Now we know who Munro is! Now, we have a means of identifying him!"

Wentworth frowned, shook his head slowly while Kirkpatrick switched on the microphone again and began barking out a general alarm for Charles Maurice.

"Get all possible pictures of him, get fingerprints from his apartment and broadcast them...."

Wentworth leaned forward sharply. "Get all possible *group* photographs of Maurice, showing him with other members of the casts for years back! Particularly in England!"

Kirkpatrick stared at Wentworth, frowning, then repeated the order into the microphone. But he was still frowning when he turned back to Wentworth.

"Confound it, Dick!" he snapped. "What are you up to now?

Today's development proves definitely that Munro and Maurice are one and the same man!"

"Munro is certainly a genius at makeup and disguise," Wentworth conceded carefully. "I'll grant that there is a close connection between Munro and Maurice!"

Kirkpatrick scowled, and his eyes were cold and speculative as they bored into Wentworth's. "No doubt," he said curtly. "The connection is close. As close as the connection between Richard Wentworth... and the Spider!"

Wentworth laughed lightly. "Why as to that, Kirk," he said. "We, the Spider and I, do have a great many things in common. Personally, I think Richard Wentworth the smarter man!"

THE PATROL which Kirkpatrick had ordered was waiting at the corner beside the Nation's Bank, and Wentworth was turned over to the police with brief instructions to make sure he stayed behind bars until Kirkpatrick returned to headquarters.

Locked inside the patrol, Wentworth waved a hand airily, "There is plenty of time, Kirk," he said. "The robbery here won't take place until the streets are crowded... and it still lacks some several hours of dawn! I'll be looking forward to your visit!"

When the patrol rolled away, Kirkpatrick was still standing, an erect uncompromising figure, and his frown refused to lighten at Wentworth's quips. He was Wentworth's closest friend, but he would brook no violation whatsoever of the laws.

If he got the evidence he sought, to prove Wentworth and the Spider one man, he would prosecute with all the drive of which he was so resolutely capable!

The patrol had traveled ten blocks before Wentworth spotted

the small coupé that was trailing. He watched it with narrowed eyes through a space of minutes, then saw another car whip around the corner and pass it. Wentworth started to his feet. There could be no doubt at all that a signal had passed between the occupants of those two cars, and now the new arrival was spurting toward the patrol with an added burst of speed!

There were three policemen on the patrol, two in the front seat, and a third seated across from Wentworth, locked in with him. The third officer whipped up his gun.

"Sit down!" he snapped.

Wentworth pointed toward the pursuing car, now almost immediately behind the patrol. "The patrol is about to be attacked," he said flatly.

The policeman looked but the car was passing the patrol. At the same instant, a spurt of flame winked from the coupé Wentworth had first noticed. A tire on the patrol exploded. The police truck lurched, and, forward, there was a crash of metal; the jangle of violently smashed glass!

Wentworth pitched to the floor. At the same instant, the policeman sprang toward him. Wentworth saw the raised black-jack, tried to dodge—and his head smacked against the wall. The blackjack jarred explosively against his skull.

Wentworth's dimming eyes stared up into the policeman's face. The devil! Was this some new trick of Munro's... His senses flicked out with that thought....

CHAPTER 6
TERROR AT HIGH NOON!

PAIN WAS Wentworth's first reminder that he still lived. He fought his way upward through tons of blackness that absorbed all his strength. Deliberately, at the end, he maintained a semblance of unconsciousness till he could gauge his surroundings. The attack on the patrol, even the policeman on guard, might well have been part of a Munro plot!

A footfall sounded lightly, close beside him, and Wentworth started to the touch of a soft hand on his forehead.

A voice called his name gently. "Dick! Can you hear me, Dick?"

Wentworth wrenched open his eyes and gazed into the face of—Nita!

He stared without comprehension for a moment. Was Nita a prisoner also? He glanced rapidly over the room, caught the smiling sardonic gaze of Ralph Warring and recognized that he was in an apartment, in an ordinary bedroom.

"The Gotham Hounds, sir," said Warring, "have snatched you from durance vile! It involved us in a bit of a struggle, but though there were some broken police heads, and a bit of material damage to a patrol wagon, that was all. I may say, prideful, that no one was killed!"

Before Warring had fairly started to speak, Wentworth realized the whole picture. His hand reached out to Nita's... and the clasp was hidden from Warring by Nita's body. He turned Nita's hand gently, looked at her wrist watch, and shock ran through

71

him. Half-past eleven! And outside, the bright warm sunlight of the spring day streamed past the windows. That blow on the head had laid him out for hours, and in that time Munro might have struck at the bank! Morning rush hour, or noon….

Nita said, gently, "There has been no attack on the bank… yet!"

With a final, soft pressure of Nita's hand, he released his hold, thrust himself up from the pillow against which he rested.

"The bank?" he snapped. "To hell with the bank! Your confounded interference has got me in bad with the police! Who asked you to pull a fool stunt like that? Nita, if you helped them…."

Nita drew herself up proudly, but there was a smile in the depths of the eyes. "Why, Dick!" she exclaimed. "We were only trying to help you! To think you'd talk to me like this!"

Wentworth swore. He was dressed except for collar and shoes. He began to fumble for them while he fought down the agony of the concussion he had suffered.

"I've got enough trouble," Wentworth said petulantly, "without having to dodge the police all the time! You, Warring, and your damned meddling friends!"

Warring was watching with a wary smile on his lips, eyes almost closed. "What did you have in mind doing, Wentworth?" he asked softly.

"Doing?" Wentworth straightened, reached for his coat. "Doing? I'm going and surrender to the police! Oh, don't worry about my reporting you! I'll say that I haven't the least idea who it was rescued me. The policeman will be bound to admit that he knocked me out with his blackjack. I woke up in a hotel room."

WENTWORTH WAS watching Warring while he spoke, trying to guess whether the man would try to prevent his departure. There was so damned little time. Without any doubt at all, Munro would strike at the bank as soon as the lunch hour crowds were thick in the streets. Before that time, the Spider must be ready!

"So you don't appreciate our efforts?" Warring murmured.

"Asinine, stupid meddling!" Wentworth shouted. "No, I don't need your help! Nita, you at least should have known better!"

Nita's head was up, and her fists knotted at her sides. "You're an ungrateful wretch!" she said indignantly. "We help you, and then you behave this way! Go on back to the police—and I hope you get a year in prison!"

Wentworth made no response to that. He strode resolutely for the door and when his back was turned to Warring, he deliberately winked at Nita! There was no change in her face, but as usual she had caught his purpose clearly. She would be invaluable to him as a spy upon the movements of the Hounds—and if they thought she had quarreled with Wentworth, they would be more inclined to trust her. Wentworth was under no illusions as to why they had snatched him from the police.

"We crave your forgiveness, Wentworth," Warring said mockingly, "but you see, we considered it would be impossible to catch the Spider while you were locked up!"

"Don't try to mend matters by flattering me!" Wentworth flung back at him, though he fully understood the implication

73

of Warring's words. Warring was telling him, clearly, that the Hounds were still convinced that Wentworth and the Spider were one and the same man!

"Nothing was farther from my mind," Warring answered, "but I insist upon driving you to police headquarters. You see, the Hounds have made me responsible for you."

"Very well, if you insist," Wentworth acknowledged quietly, "but it will have to be fast. And if the police capture me, in your company, before I have surrendered, it will be disastrous for you!"

There was no more conversation while they entered Warring's car and drove rapidly toward headquarters. Nita rode with them, but held herself coldly aloof. Warring's lips were set in their perpetually mocking smile, and Wentworth was preoccupied. He stole a covert glance at clocks they passed. This was causing an endless delay, but it would have its value also. Warring would be able to testify that he had brought Wentworth to police headquarters—and if he handled matters well, that fact might set up an alibi for the Spider!

At the curb before police headquarters, Wentworth sprang to the walk. Without a word to Nita, or to Warring, he ran up the steps and into the main hallway. He knew the geography of headquarters perfectly, and he angled swiftly for a rear exit, while he kept his head bowed as if in thought, altered his usually alert stride against recognition by officers he passed. Within fifteen minutes, a half hour at most, Munro would strike at the Nation's Bank—and the Spider must be there to greet him!

IT WAS at the same moment when Wentworth was hurrying through the halls of police headquarters, that a limousine slid to

the curb before the Nation's Bank and
an oldish man alighted somewhat stiffly
with the chauffeur's help. His shoulders,
beneath the perfect fit of a cutaway, were
stooped and his silver hair crisped out
beneath the brim of his silk hat.

"Return about three, Francis," he
said. "Oh, yes, bring that satchel into
my office."

The chauffeur saluted, "Yes, Mr.
Oldham."

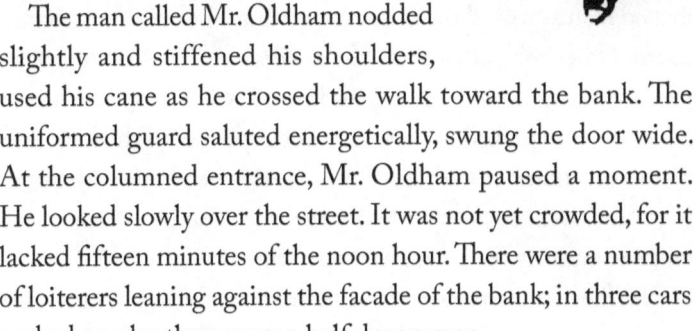

The man called Mr. Oldham nodded
slightly and stiffened his shoulders,
used his cane as he crossed the walk toward the bank. The
uniformed guard saluted energetically, swung the door wide.
At the columned entrance, Mr. Oldham paused a moment.
He looked slowly over the street. It was not yet crowded, for it
lacked fifteen minutes of the noon hour. There were a number
of loiterers leaning against the facade of the bank; in three cars
parked nearby, there were a half dozen men.

The guard leaned forward respectfully, "Those are the extra
police guards, sir," he whispered. "And there are lots more out
of sight! Inside, too!"

Mr. Oldham nodded gravely, walked deliberately across
the lobby. The door to the inner mysteries buzzed open at his
approach, and an official hurried toward him.

"Oh, sir, you shouldn't have come down today!"

Mr. Oldham smiled. "Nonsense, man. Nonsense; there is no

danger with all the police on guard! Set the satchel in my office, Francis, then you may go."

The eyes, keen behind rimless spectacles, watched narrowly as Francis swung the satchel to the floor. It jarred heavily, and Mr. Oldham stiffened, a little apprehensively. But nothing happened; Francis saluted once more, and marched out of the bank. Mr. Oldham strolled on into his office.

"I shan't want to be disturbed," he murmured back over his shoulder.

As the door swung shut. Mr. Oldham swung about with an extraordinary alertness for so old a man. He sprang to the door, locked it and crossed the office to peer into the connected bathroom. No other door there. He nodded his head in approval, plucked up the heavy satchel and eased it down on top of the desk. Then he picked up a private direct phone on the desk and spun out a number with a stiffened forefinger. Presently, buzzing came over the wire. When it had sounded three times, and without waiting for an answer, he hung up.

He dialed another number. Six times, his head bent forward with every indication of alert youthfulness, he performed that task, and each time he hung up without waiting for an answer. Afterward, he sat rigidly, eyes fixed on a small bronze clock on the desk. Minutes ticked past slowly, and the hands stood at three before twelve when the man the staff greeted as "Mr. Oldham" began to smile. It was a slow smile, wolfish, cruel, and greedy.

The little bronze clock had begun to glow. It threw off a faint, cold, greenish light!

Mr. Oldham stood and opened his satchel. From it, he took a light metal diving helmet. Rapidly, he settled it over his shoulders. Then he dipped again into the satchel, and, one by one, he took out six glass spheres. They were transparent, and within them green vapors swirled like filthy roiled waters. Mr. Oldham handled them very carefully and set them in a neat little row upon his desk. Afterward, he sat down and folded his hands. Through the vision window in the front of the helmet, his face showed dimly. That wolfish smile was widening on his lips.

The clock on the desk showed one minute of twelve. The green glow was vivid now. It quivered and sent out streamers of light.

Under the helmet, Mr. Oldham chuckled.

THE FIRST eager rush of the luncheon crowd was streaming out into the street. The elevators were pumping out a rapid flow of humanity. The sound of their hurrying feet, of their lifting, liberated voices beat into the office where Mr. Oldham sat. His hand moved caressingly to the green globes....

The police guards in the cars, on the roofs, were conscious of a mounting tension. They had been at their posts throughout the morning. The blow had not fallen in the rush hour, and this was the second danger point according to their instructions. The sidewalks were getting jammed. Auto traffic was a crawling snake amid an ocean of people that overflowed into the streets.

In one of the watch cars, Mike Finnegan shifted restlessly. "Hell of a note," he grumbled to his partner, Al Haines. "How much longer we got to wait? My innards feel empty!"

Al laughed. "That ain't hunger. You're just plain scared!" he said. His laughter didn't seem quite natural and it cut off.

Mike looked at him. "Look," he said, "do you feel… scared, too?"

Al shifted in his seat. "Not exactly *scared,*" he said, and then, looking at Mike, his eyes widened. "Hey, Mike! Lookit your shield!"

Mike pulled down his broad chin, and stared at his half-hidden shield under his lapel. His face lost its high color. Al's voice was curious and flat. "Orders say: 'Look for danger if your shield begins to glow with a green light!'"

Mike swore, thinly. "It's green, or I'm a Dutchman!"

Al tried to laugh. He felt cold and quivering inside. "You ain't no Dutchman, Mike!"

THE TWO girls were clattering along on their high heels, their voices high, a little shrill, but happy as they hesitated before a shop window.

"Come payday, Agnes, I'm buying me those!" One pointed to a froth of silken underwear.

Agnes shrugged. "They're pretty, but me, Lil, I'm holding on to my cash."

Lil twisted her blondined head around. "You! Holding onto cash! What you scared of?"

Agnes didn't answer her at once. They stood and looked at each other without speaking. Agnes' shoulder shivered a little, and she looked behind her.

"I don't know," she said, in a muffled voice. "But I am… scared!"

Lil said, "Ah, don't be so silly!" She didn't sound happy, and she didn't look again at the silk underwear in the window. She was looking at Agnes, and her eyes had a strange light. "Funny," she said. "Your beads got a funny sort of green shine to them."

Agnes shivered again. "Look, let's go eat."

They started across the street toward the Nation's Bank corner. There was a street cleaner in a white suit, with a wheeled cart and a long-handled brush, in their way, and they started around him. The man glanced at them, and his eyes were gray-blue and keen. His gaze drew to sharp focus on the beads that Agnes wore and his lips made a tight, straight line across his face.

"You girls better get off the street, quickly!" he told them quietly.

The two girls stared at him, and didn't answer, and hurried on toward the bank corner. The street cleaner swore under his breath. His long-handled brush clanged against the cart. On the sidewalk, a man started nervously at the sound.

"Damn you!" he rasped. "Do you have to do that?"

In Mr. Oldham's office, the man in the helmet got to his feet and picked up two of the glass spheres....

THERE WASN'T much laughing now in the street crowds. People moved hurriedly, with a jerky nervousness and quick over-shoulder glances. Voices were muted when anyone spoke at all, and the clatter and thud of swift heels was the dominant note. The narrow walls caught the sound and imprisoned it, as if they, too, conspired with the terror that was breeding here. They would not let even the sound escape.

When people collided, they shied apart with paling faces, or quick, reasonless anger. Footsteps, suddenly behind a man, could make him whirl like an animal at bay. In their cars, the police were bolt upright, and their eyes held the trapped, despairing look of men at zero hour of a hopeless assault.

The street cleaner clutched his long brush and wheeled the cart toward the bank. His face was pallid; his hands made clenched white fists. His steps were deliberate and stiff, as if all his muscles were braced in titanic effort. His eyes quested everywhere, spotted a car loaded with men which forced its way through the flow of pedestrians to a halt before a small jewelry store. More police? Perhaps... still they might be killers!

He stared at them fixedly, saw how men darted in abrupt terror from their path. That was why he didn't see a window in the bank ease open. It opened only a few inches, perhaps six. The glass spheres were only three inches in diameter....

The window made a small creaking sound, and two girls on the sidewalk muffled their brief cries of fear and grabbed each other convulsively.

"Oh, Lil!" one sobbed. "Oh, look. Inside that window. A man in a... in a helmet!"

The two girls turned up white, terrified faces, and something flew through the air toward them from that partly opened window, something that glittered in a stream of warm sunlight; a dark, green sphere with a sheen like old bronze. Yes, very lovely in the sunlight....

The girls were frozen in their fear. Screams crowded up from their swelling throats, came out shrill and hoarse and terrible with fear; beat against the imprisoning walls of stone, and racketed up into the clear warmth of the day, fluttered in the ears of the crowd that terror rode.

That was before the sphere reached them.

Agnes saw the sphere coming, lovely and glisten-

• *NITA VAN SLOAN* •

ing, floating toward her. She thrust out a wild, rigid hand to check it and it just brushed her fingers. It struck against her forehead. Not a hard blow; a drifting balloon would have been almost as heavy. It was enough to break the glass. Agnes felt a minute burn as a fragile sliver bit into her forehead. Something green and greasy like coal smoke eddied down before her eyes. It laid its tendrils against her cheeks.

Beside her, Lil was screaming again and again as quickly as she could draw breath. She stood very still, and the tendrils were reaching for her, too. They seemed gentle and caressing; they had an especial affinity for warm young flesh. They twined and coiled against it.

There was just an instant when the screams stopped; when they burst out again, they were incredible. They were horror and terror, but they were more than that. They were sheer, animal agony!

IT HAD happened in a space of heart-beats, but when finally Agnes and Lil burst the bonds of their paralytic fear; when they turned to flee from the pain that they could not leave behind them, their hands thrust out blindly before them. They ran, and they struck against an automobile, and did not see it. They burst out into the street and other screams ran before them, men's and women's, as they stampeded like a herd of terror-maddened cattle. For Agnes and Lil were no longer human beings. Their faces were gleaming white, skeleton skulls!

In the car against which they crashed, two men sat rigidly, realizing that the thing they had been waiting for had struck. Al Haines twisted toward those awful skull faces, and beyond him, Mike Finnegan's lips burst apart in a strange mixture of curse and prayer. They were trembling with their fear, but they were policemen. They pulled out their guns, and leaped to the pavement. And another glass sphere sailed majestically through the air to greet them.

Afterward, there were two men also who ran screaming along that already panic-stricken street, beings with the bodies of men, but with faces that were the nightmare faces of Death!

More swiftly than ran those dying men and women, terror swept through the crowded street. Nameless fears had made them cold and empty within, and now in these screams that tore the air to shreds, they felt the fulfillment of their baseless apprehensions. But there was no tangible thought. An electric tension crackled over their heads, joined them fellow to fellow, in a thoughtless, emotion-ridden throng.

The street cleaner had whipped about with the first cry from the girls, and he saw the bursting of that first green sphere. Instantly, his white coat was torn open. His hands vanished to his armpits and when they reappeared, they glinted with the ominous black metal of guns. For the moment, there was no target. He could not have seen the source of that floating green sphere. He stood, feeling the terror that drained every soul about him, feeling it shake his brain and body. But he did not yield.

Not even when the stampede burst… and he saw the source of the second bomb!

Instantly, the guns flamed in his fists! Two neat holes punched through the partly opened window of the bank; glass cascaded to the pavement. Behind it, was only the emptiness of an office neatly paneled in wood. No one was in sight.

The man in white whirled toward the trash can, reached into its depths. When he straightened, a long black cape swirled from his shoulders, and low upon his brows, was a broad-brimmed black hat. The black guns in his fists were ominous as death. No man who looked now could fail to recognize him. The Spider raced into battle!

CHAPTER 7
THE FACE OF DEATH!

E VEN AS the Spider straightened, there was a crashing of gunshots, and two men dashed out of the jewelry shop across the street toward the parked car which waited, motor racing, at the curb!

The Spider laughed, and the flat mockery of the sound pierced even through the terrified screams of the mob. He saw a woman, running wildly, collide with one of the gunmen; saw the killer snarl and twist about with a gun!

The Spider's right-hand automatic recoiled in his fist and the gunman jerked up on his toes, all his body tightening in the onslaught of death! His companion made a wild leap for the car, and it was already moving. It gathered speed, sweeping toward the crowd that packed the street from side to side. A gun blasted from the car, and the crouching Spider heard the bullet's hungry whine. Once more his automatic spoke and the crook who clung to the running board twisted with a scream. One hand clung frantically to the car, but his body arched backward, and he pin-wheeled to the pavement. His head struck with a cracking sound.

In the same instant, the Spider sent the street cleaner's cart scooting across the pavement. The driver of the getaway car saw it coming, but already he had picked up fierce speed. He tried to swerve, and the cart crashed against his radiator. It was ground beneath the fender, caught beneath the front wheel. The car leaped the curb, buried its hood in a shop window. The Spider's gun spoke once more. After that, there was no movement and no sound from the inside of the wrecked car.

Wentworth straightened up and faced warily about. Where men and women had jammed all the street, only a few moments before, there were only the remnants of a vanishing crowd. The police cars stood deserted against the curb. In the street lay the crushed bodies of those who had been ground beneath trampling feet.

Wentworth's face had an unearthly whiteness. The fists that gripped his guns were rigid as stone, and the line of his jaw was traced in white. He was riven by the fear he could not explain, that roweled him with as cruel spurs as had goaded these others into frantic flight. Only the mighty will of him who was known as the Master of Men gave him control against the wild urge to stampede with the others. That explained why he moved so slowly as he moved toward the doors of the Nation's Bank. He did not even trust himself to run, lest the terror gain control of his limbs over the domination of his mind!

A man and woman, both dead, lay upon the stone steps of the bank. The woman's face was… gone.

WENTWORTH'S EYES lifted fiercely toward the bank doors. He weighed the automatics in his fist. He plunged up the steps!

The black cape swirled out from his shoulders, and anger burned coldly in his eyes. His shoulder struck aside the swinging glass door, and he plunged into the bank!

For that first instant, just inside the portals, he stood motionless. Death was all about him. A bank guard and two civilians were sprawled upon the floor There was no other human thing in sight; nothing that had been human. As he stood there a gun spoke!

Wentworth felt the shock of the lead in his left hand, and his right-hand gun blasted out its answer the same instant. He dived toward the cover of the marble counter from behind which the shot had come. There was a tingling numbness that ran from his left hand to his shoulder, but the arm answered the demand of his brain. It caught him as he struck on his chest, and rolled against the front of the counter.

He lay there, breathless through a long moment, waiting. He saw something that glittered toward him in a brilliant arc. And he knew the menace that promised! Munro and his devils were here. That was a gas bomb, such as would devour a man's face!

Wentworth's gun kicked in his fist and, half the length of the bank's concourse away, the glass globe met the bullet in mid-air. The green gas spread like a parachute in the air, settled in slow, coiling tentacles toward the floor. For the moment, Wentworth was safe. It would take several seconds for those tendrils to reach him. Before then, he must move. He slid like a snake... toward the spot where the gas was settling.

It was the one thing that Munro would not expect, and Wentworth moved fast. It was not until now that he could glance toward his left hand; it was uninjured. By some trick of luck, Munro's bullet had only struck the gun from the Spider's fist! But it had been his fully loaded automatic; only two bullets remained in the other, and there was no chance to reload as he raced to pass that slowly drifting gas before it should reach the floor!

Behind him, he heard the fragile spat of another bomb striking the floor. If he had retreated, he would have been defenseless, caught by the gas that devoured human flesh! But he was losing his race against the gas tentacles ahead! They were settling more rapidly! Wentworth got his feet beneath him, and once more plunged forward in a dive. His eyes strained upward to watch the green spirals of death. The eddy of his passage whirled them toward him, and he flung himself to his feet, sprinted!

A gun blasted again and again, hammering lead at him. He whirled and flung up his automatic. There was his enemy, crouched behind a desk! The man's revolver jumped as he pumped lead as fast as a finger could squeeze the trigger! Wentworth's mocking laughter rang out; he dropped his automatic into line. Against the dazzle of a window, he could only make out the curved line of the head and the leveled gun; but it would be enough!

The Spider laughed... and squeezed off his last two shots!

Instantly, the gunfire was silenced. The hunched outline of the head was smacked down behind the desk!

"Munro!" Wentworth cried. "Munro, you're finished!"

With a shout, he bounded toward the desk. His gun was a club in his fist, and triumph was hot in his throat. With a long leap, Wentworth cleared the desk… and a cry lifted in his throat. On the floor lay a helmet with a fractured vision glass; with a bullet dent upon the forehead. But of the man who had worn it, of Munro—there was no trace at all!

WENTWORTH STOOD, staring vacantly down at the helmet. Through the windows of the bank, light streamed in and laid a sunny bar across the casque of steel. It was that sunlight which, for the moment, saved Wentworth's life. A shadow flickered across it, and Wentworth lunged straight forward a full ten feet! Behind him, he heard a gasped oath, heard the vicious crunch of wood yielding beneath a titan's blow.

The Spider whirled, and at a distance of a few yards, he was staring into the hate-maddened eyes of Munro! Munro still clutched the haft of a fire-axe which was driven deep into the desk beside which, a moment before, Wentworth had stood!

Through a long heartbeat of time, the two enemies regarded each other, Munro in the silvery wig, the formal garments of President Oldham of the Nation's Bank, shoulders arched with a power that belied the age of his make-up as he wrenched the axe free. Wentworth was upright, the cape graceful from his broad shoulders, triumph in the eager up-fling of his head. Face-to-face at last with Munro! It was a moment he had dreamed of, and he would not fail!

Wentworth's right hand whipped back, and he flung the empty gun at Munro's face! He leaped to the attack, his hands reaching out eagerly, fingers curled for a strangle hold upon the throat of this mass murderer of the innocent!

But Munro was ready for him. He made no attempt to dodge the gun, but interposed the haft of his axe. The heavy automatic glanced from the wood, clattered futilely to the floor. Munro stood on braced legs, powerful shoulders taut as he heaved the axe high above his head with both arms. He was laughing, deep in his chest, and the happiness of this murder gleamed in his eyes. Then the axe flashed down!

Even in that desperate instant, Wentworth did not lose his head. He swayed out from under that axe like a boxer, thrust up a stiffened left arm toward the axe, as a fencer turns aside a powerful lunge.

The axe haft struck the back of his left wrist and Wentworth stiffened that arm in a frantic effort to make the axe glance aside. He might have succeeded completely, but in that crucial moment, his foot slipped. Down he went to one knee.

The haft glanced against Wentworth's skull. The blade, turned by Wentworth's swift thrust, struck flat across his shoulders and drove him to the floor. In that instant, as he fell, Wentworth reached up and set both hands upon the handle of the axe and… hung on.

The bank spun about him in a dizzy whirl, and there was a blackness inside his skull that made Munro's face appear in little flashes of green light. He dully felt the impact of Munro's kicks raining against his ribs, of fists hammering at his face. And he hung on to the axe.

Despite the murderous assault, his senses were beginning to clear, but all his muscles would not rouse to do his will. He realized that Munro's face had steadied above him, and that there was pain in his throat. Munro had given up the struggle for the axe. Munro was… strangling him!

WENTWORTH TRIED to drive his heavy body into action. It should be simple to break this hold, to roll Munro from his perch. But the grip of those murderous hands upon his throat swelled the agony within his skull. Munro's face floated above his own. The eyes burned down gloatingly, and the murder lust distorted even the careful disguise of old kind Oldham. The pressure of those deadly hands was increasing.

"Fool!" Munro panted. "Fool to think that you can destroy Munro! This is how I've always wanted to kill you, with my own hands! Slowly, as you deserve to die!"

Wentworth's brain seemed to take on a feverish clarity as his breath was pinched off. He had not the strength to throw off this murderer, but there still was a way… a possible way. If only, for a space of seconds, he could loosen one of these hands from his throat!

Wentworth's left hand was ground down into his side by the weight of Munro's body, but it was close to his vest pocket and that was what he wanted. If only… Ah! His fingers closed about the slim cigarette lighter that he always carried there, and somehow he wrenched it free of Munro's weight. His thumb clicked against the base, sprung it open. This was no sinister weapon, but there was a secret hidden in its base. Wentworth lifted it feebly, and set that base against the fist Munro clamped about his throat.

Then Wentworth heard Munro swear. Wentworth could not see it, but on the back of Munro's right hand, there glowed a crimson design… *the seal of the Spider!*

Munro swore, and the hand wrenched away from Wentworth's throat! It was the moment for which Wentworth had gambled. He jerked up on the axe, which lay upon his chest, and there was a cry of agony from Munro. He pitched to the floor, and Wentworth struggled to his feet. The axe seemed to weigh a ton in his hand as he attempted to raise it. But Munro, though he was bent double in pain, was scrambling away.

Wentworth tried to throw the axe, and it slipped from his hands. Munro was moving more rapidly now. He stopped and caught up a heavy satchel and darted along behind the marble counter toward the main doors! Wentworth tried to run after him, and his feet played him tricks. He stumbled and fell, caught at a desk with both hands. Munro was leaving!

Then Wentworth laughed drunkenly. He reached out with both hands and seized a telephone instrument and, as he reeled to his feet, he threw himself backward. The telephone pulled loose from its fastenings. He gripped the wires and swung the heavy handset around his head like a slingshot!

Munro reached the door, stooped for the gun that Wentworth had dropped. The wires of the phone were whistling over Wentworth's head. As Munro straightened, Wentworth let the phone fly.

The phone did not miss.

It struck Munro across the side of his skull and drove him to his knees. The gun skittered out from under his hand, the satchel dropped from his fingers. Then he pitched crashing forward on his face!

WENTWORTH FELT a shout of triumph swell in his chest, but it came out weakly. He reeled away from the marble railing, started forward, still dazed. He could not take the most direct path, for the gas huddled in little green clots before him.

Wentworth was laughing, weakly, as he moved toward the door circuitously. He had won. He had downed Munro when he least expected it. If only he could reach him now before he recovered. The lighter was still in his left hand, and he laughed at it. That little thing! Munro had feared its symbolism, more than the seal itself; but he had feared, too, to have it printed upon his dead body. Now, as always, Munro wore a disguise. But the seal could never be eradicated. Fear of the Spider had beaten Munro in the end. It....

Wentworth came to an incredulous halt behind the teller's cages. He was staring toward where Munro had fallen. The gun lay there, and the satchel that plainly contained the loot of the bank. But of Munro, there was no trace at all!

A cry burst from Wentworth's lips. He reeled forward in a fumbling run. A trail of spattered bloodrops led toward the front door!

Desperately, Wentworth snatched up his gun and drove his dragging body toward the broad portals of the bank. Munro could not escape him now! Dazed though Wentworth was,

Munro must be equally injured after the savage impact of that telephone! If only he could overtake him, and....

Wentworth reeled out of the door. His cape swirled bravely behind him. His hat had been knocked off, and his hair sprawled across the high whiteness of his forehead. His eyes were fierce. He staggered to a halt on the steps, braced himself... and guns blasted at him from across the street—three different guns! Wentworth's own automatic jumped upward in his hand, ready, and then he rasped out an oath.

Munro was not in sight, but he knew the three men across the street. They were the Gotham Hounds!

Frantically, Wentworth hurled himself backward through the doors in the same instant the crash of bullets sent the glass of the panels cascading to the floor. Damn it, Munro must still be inside the bank—but no! There ran the trail of blood! Then, Munro was making good his escape while the Hounds covered his retreat by keeping the Spider prisoner in the bank!

Anger curled Wentworth's lips. Were the Gotham Hounds allies of Munro? He could not be sure. But Wentworth the Spider, did not shoot men on suspicion! He must escape to find Munro.

Wentworth thrust himself out from the wall against which he leaned. His strength was flowing back through his limbs now, and he walked with more confidence. But, even as he neared a window, he heard the multiple shrieks of sirens, saw blue-coated men spilling from squad cars to the pavement beneath the very window from which he sought to escape.

Wentworth dodged back into the obscurity of the bank's

interior, and he cursed savagely. The Gotham Hounds had run the Spider to earth!

IT WAS only a few brief minutes later that the police charged in through the doorway. Behind them crept the three Hounds, guns in their fists.

"He's in here!" Hunter cried, in his deep booming voice. "We drove him back when he was trying to kill the president of the bank! And the place has been surrounded ever since!"

The police crept forward through the doorway, and swore as their eyes quested over the floor. Sprawled upon the white pavement were huge words.

"Beware green stuff! Poison gas!"

It was signed with the Spider's seal!

But of the Spider himself, there was no sign at all for that long first moment. Then one of the policemen spoke.

"There!" he cried. "There behind the desk!"

Bullets poured from his gun toward a hunched, be-caped figure, wearing a helmet, that crouched behind a desk. There was a gun in the hand, but apparently the policeman's first bullets took effect, for he did not fire. The guns of the entire squad were spitting out their drum roll of death. A sub-machine gun added its mad chatter. They were all inside the bank, even the Hounds. Hunter held his post beside the door, but he did not notice the man dressed in white who sprawled face down where blood stained the white floor. He did not notice the man rise to his feet. The first warning he had was when the muzzle of a gun dug into his kidney!

"All right, Hunter," whispered the cold voice in his ear. "Back into this entry now! That's right! Now, stoop! You're going to carry me out of the bank and into an ambulance! Stoop, you yellow hound!"

Hunter shivered, bent his shoulders and the man in white threw his weight across them… as the gun continued to dig into Hunter's side.

"All right, Hunter," whispered the same voice. "Now, carry me to the ambulance! If you hesitate you're a dead man!"

Hunter stumbled down the steps, and a voice that sounded hoarsely like his own, called out for an ambulance. The police opened a way for him, and Hunter scrambled into the ambulance with his burden. The ambulance got under way.…

It was several hours before the protesting Hounds accompanied Kirkpatrick back to headquarters.

"Damn it," Hunter was insisting. "What could I do, with a gun in my back? As soon as we got inside the ambulance, he knocked me out. After that, I don't know what happened. And I don't know who it was! It might have been Munro, or it might have been the Spider! But I'm almost sure it was the Spider."

Kirkpatrick said grimly, "We'll take your statement down, Hunter."

Laird's voice was cold, "What I want to know is this: Where has Wentworth been all this time?"

Kirkpatrick thrust open the door of his office, and a curse rasped from his lips. He strode across the threshold and then slowly, very slowly, he smiled.

"Apparently," he said, and nodded toward the man who slept,

sprawled across Kirkpatrick's desk. "Apparently, Wentworth has been catching a bit of rest in my private office!"

HE CROSSED softly to where Wentworth's head rested on folded arms and, carefully, touched a finger to the throat pulse. He nodded slowly. Wentworth was really very sound asleep.

He shook Wentworth's shoulder. "When did you get here?" he snapped. "Come on! Talk up! When did you get here?"

Wentworth's head snapped up, and he started sharply to his feet. He shook off Kirkpatrick's hand irritably.

"That's a hell of a way to wake a man up," he said. "You keep lousy office hours, Kirk. I've been waiting for hours to surrender."

"Hours?" Kirkpatrick asked drily.

Wentworth nodded sharply. "Exactly. I see it's dusk now, and it was broad daylight when I came here. Ask Warring, he saw me enter!"

Warring's smile was mocking, and he delayed speech while all eyes centered on his face. He nodded finally. "Quite so," he said, "and I did better than that. I took a picture of him going into the building, and there's a clock in the background. I think it may be accepted as evidence."

Kirkpatrick nodded gravely. "I'm taking no more chances with you, Dick," he said curtly. "You're going into a cell right now. I'll question you later about your escape from that patrol wagon."

Wentworth smiled and shrugged. "It won't help you, Kirk," he said. "If you question the officer who was inside with me, he'll tell you that he knocked me cold just when the crash occurred. He'll know more about it than I do!"

Kirkpatrick nodded, took his seat behind the desk. Wentworth studied his face impassively. The lines about the mouth were drawn and deep, and sitting wearily, Kirkpatrick dragged a knuckle across his pointed mustache. Wentworth knew his friend was deeply worried. His gesture as he indicated chairs for the three Hounds was infinitely tired. But Wentworth had no chance to hear what was said, or to learn the reason for the three men being brought to headquarters. Two police officers came and, with drawn guns, escorted him to a cell. The clanging of the door was sullen and heavy, and Wentworth dropped to the cot bed. He would be able to force arraignment and release on bail the next day. He thought that Munro would remain idle for this night at least. He had suffered a serious defeat, despite the early success of his plans. He had been forced to abandon the loot— important as evidence. Tomorrow, then… Wentworth forced rest upon his mind, blanking out the horror of the day's battling.

IN HIS office, Kirkpatrick rested his elbows on the desk, knotted his long fingers together as he bent his regard on the three men. Laird, as usual, was sitting bolt upright, while Warring lounged with a camera slung across his chest. Hunter, his head bandaged, had his knees crossed jauntily, his chin lifted in his perpetual challenge.

"This evidence concerning Wentworth," said Kirkpatrick slowly, "does not change your verdict, gentlemen?"

Laird shook his head crisply. "We can identify the Spider," he said, "if you will exhibit him to us in the same garments, under conditions similar to those at the theatre. We all had a good look at him then, and we have trained memories. Warring had pictures also, but he was unfortunately knocked out and robbed of his camera."

"My favorite one, too," Warring sighed.

Kirkpatrick nodded crisply. "Very well," he said. "I will act upon your evidence. There is the possibility that the Spider is such a… gentleman as yourselves, but he is known to masquerade in the Underworld, also." Kirkpatrick flipped a cam in the annunciator on his desk. "Sergeant Reams, request Captain Fillarty to assign me six of his best men; those who have the widest knowledge of underworld characters. I want them at once."

When the six men filed into his office, Kirkpatrick rose and faced them, outlined the prospects of identifying the Spider.

"Here is what I want," he ended crisply. "The Spider is known to appear periodically in the underworld in the guise of a crook. He would be a man well known to other criminals, under the masquerade of course. He would be a man who made his appearance in New York usually at the time of some such series of crimes as confronts us now. His reputation is that he always works alone, and must pull some good jobs because he never lacks for money. He may, or may not, have a reputation as a skillful safe cracker. Can you name any crook who fits into that pattern?"

The six detectives looked at each other, concentrated frowningly on the picture. A few names were offered hesitantly. Bosco Smutts, a con man who was supposed to travel a lot; Flash Davis, who was suspected of staging bank robberies over a wide range of territory.

It was the big grizzled detective with a birthmark on his right cheek who snapped his fingers in sudden discovery.

"By the lord Harry, commissioner," he said. "I've got the man who fits the bill all the way down to safe cracking, and the time of his appearance. Those other guys, I can't time them with your big crime waves, but this mug I can. He never seems to run out of money. I don't think he's smart enough to be the Spider. Otherwise, he fits all right."

Kirkpatrick nodded. "All right, Grogan. Who is he?"

Grogan hesitated, nodded. "Well he fits, all right. You may not know him. It's a half-blind peterman named Blinky McQuade!"

The door of Kirkpatrick's office was suddenly batted open, and Captain Fillarty, of the detective bureau, bounded into the room.

"Commissioner!" he rasped. "That damned Munro has struck again! He took a savings bank up town that has night banking hours. Had four guys with him! They threw those damned gas bombs, cleaned up about fifteen thousand bucks… and they killed eight people!"

Kirkpatrick rasped out a harsh oath. "We'll get up there right away!" He swung toward the six detectives. "You understand your orders! Get those three men, and any others that fit into the pattern. And above all, get McQuade!"

CHAPTER 8
THE TRAP FOR BLINKY

C OMMISSIONER KIRKPATRICK'S orders to the detectives were deliberately secret, so there was no possible way that Wentworth could have known about the search for Blinky McQuade, suspected of being the Spider.

That was one reason why Wentworth, as soon as he could arrange for release in bail, proceeded to disguise himself as Blinky McQuade!

It is doubtful that, even had Wentworth know of the dragnet search for Blinky, he would have chosen any other method. Through the masquerade as Blinky, he could gain entrance and hearing in the Underworld, where he had taken care to be well known. And he needed information fast!

So Wentworth raced to a certain private garage as soon as he could make sure he was not being followed. Over a secret cache beneath the floor, he knelt and undertook the rapid makeup of Blinky McQuade. He was even more careful than usual, because the man he must approach was a clever crook and, Wentworth suspected, a stool pigeon. There must never be any suspicion on the part of the police that Blinky McQuade was not just what he seemed!

Presently, Wentworth backed the battered old coupé with the secretly powerful motor beneath the hood, out of the garage. It was not possible to recognize the dapper clubman in this grizzled oldster with the iron-gray hair, the sloppy, poorly cut clothing, whose eyes seemed weak behind thick, hooded spectacles. He drove rapidly northward through the city, only stopping once. He hobbled into a corner drug store and put in a call for Nita's home.

Her voice came anxiously over the phone. "Oh, Dick!" she cried, "I hated not being there this morning when you were arraigned, but you seemed to want me to pretend a quarrel...."

"You did just right, dear," Wentworth assured her. "Those Gotham Hounds, as they call themselves, have some plan of campaign against me that I want to learn!"

Nita's laughter came to him trillingly over the phone and the taut lines of Wentworth's face relaxed. He felt the soothing release that Nita could always bring about.

"That Ralph Warring," Nita said, "fancies he has made a conquest. He's most anxious to impress me, and we're having tea this afternoon. He hinted at some special knowledge of the Spider! I know they're up to something!"

"Don't endanger yourself," Wentworth said quietly. "Dear, if you haven't heard from me by evening, I want you to go to Kirkpatrick with some information!"

"You're going into danger, Dick!" Nita interrupted.

Wentworth laughed softly. "Is that something new, Nita? No—don't interrupt. Listen. I'm convinced that Munro kidnapped the actor Maurice because he had need of more makeup skill than he himself possesses, or because he needed to train some additional men in such impersonations as he himself achieves. I think the latter. For this work, he would need to use crooks, and I'm sure the type he would use would be drawn from the more intelligent criminals, say confidence men; and he would necessarily choose the fancy dressers, since such men exhibit a certain dramatic art even in choosing clothing. These fancy-dressing con men would probably be absent from the city just now, and would have disappeared either just before, or just after, Maurice himself. I think Kirk would do well to check up on that theory. But hold it up until, say, six o'clock."

"I understand, Dick," Nita said quietly, "and it seems a sound deduction, but—Oh, Dick, be careful!"

Wentworth's lips softened in a smile. "I'm always careful, dear!" he said. "I remember that you are waiting! Goodbye!"

Back in his car, Wentworth steered westward toward the apartment of Gabby Weismann. He was almost certain to find the small-time crook at home. He hoped that he would be alone....

WENTWORTH'S TRIUMPH over Munro the day before had given way to day to despondency, since he had heard of Munro's raid on the small suburban bank. Yet, there was some consolation in the crime. It proved that Munro was desperate for money, since the fifteen thousand he had seized would ordinarily be unimportant to Munro. And since he had taken allies, he had left himself open to the methods that Wentworth would use to trace him! Very little happened in the Underworld that the grapevine did not soon carry—and Gabby was an excellent listener!

Wentworth was fortunate, for Gabby was alone when he rang at the crook's door. Gabby Weismann immediately held out a grubby hand.

"Well, well, well!" he caroled. "Where you been keeping yourself, Blinky? Geez, I ain't heard of you in ages! What do you know?"

Blinky McQuade grunted sourly, and stumped across the threshold, picked out the softest chair and eased himself into it, with his stiff leg thrust out before him.

"What you asking for?" Wentworth asked in Blinky's harsh voice. "So you can tell the cops?"

Gabby drew himself up stiffly in the purple silk dressing robe he wore. He prepared to be angry, and then he saw by the sour smile on Blinky's face that this was supposed to be a joke. Gabby laughed, and slapped his thin leg.

"By God, Blinky," he gasped, "you had me fooled!"

Wentworth let the sour smile stay on Blinky McQuade's loose lips, but he seemed in no hurry to talk. In fact, there was some embarrassment in the way he fumbled his hands between his knees. Gabby Weismann watched him with bright, small eyes.

"What's up, Blinky?" he asked. "You ain't used to paying social calls on me."

McQuade snarled, "Any law against it? Now wait… wait a minute, Gabby. I got a favor to ask of you, only I'm paying for it, see?"

Gabby guffawed. "You paying for something, Blinky!"

McQuade hobbled to his feet. "Okay, okay, Gabby!"

But the small man was immediately placating. Gabby patted his hands against Wentworth's chest. "Now just take it easy, Blinky," he said. "I didn't mean nothing by it, honest!"

"Saying I ain't got money!" Wentworth's tone sounded savage.

"I got plenty!" He hauled out a packet of bills and waved it under Gabby's nose. "I got plenty, I have! Think I'm a punk?"

Gabby's eyes strained wide at sight of the thick roll. He licked his thin lips. "Geez, there must be ten grand in that roll!" he said. "What'd you do Blinky? Knock over a bank?"

Wentworth let himself appear pacified. "That's my business," he said shortly. "Look here, Gabby. Here's the lay. Crowd I'm traveling with now is all nifty dressers, see. Now, you know I ain't never been much for duds."

Gabby giggled, thought better of it and drew a long face when Wentworth scowled at him suspiciously.

"But a slick lad like you, now," Wentworth went on stubbornly. "You know where I can get some flashy clothes without paying too much for them. And I'll make it worth your while. You can always use a new suit, can't you, Gabby?"

GABBY'S SMALL dark eyes were snapping with curiosity. "Sure," he said. "Sure, I can always use another suit. Look, Blinky, who's this flashy crowd you're playing around with now, hunh? They must be big time."

Wentworth let his lips grin sourly. "Well, they ain't small time," he admitted modestly. "Who you think?"

Gabby fairly danced with curiosity. "Well, ain't no jobs been pulled here would get you ten grand for your share. Some guy bungled the Nation's Bank here. Must of been out-of-town. Sure. Now, who's the flashy dressers ain't been around lately? Hummm. Now, there's Fancy Wade. There's Handsome Kelly. They're heist men."

Wentworth shook his head; behind his glasses, his eyes were

keen. This was the reason for his call; this was the information he wanted. "Not heist men," he said. "Slicker lads than bank boosters."

"Got you!" Gabby snapped. "Slick Marshall was one of them! He's in the money, and he just got back in town. Put himself up at the Gotham Arms!"

Wentworth snarled, "That's enough funny business now! I ain't talking. Now listen, I'll be back by here in a couple of hours, and you be ready to help me pick some fancy duds, get me, Gabby? And if anything leaks, I'm going to putt you out from between your ears!"

Gabby grinned, winked wisely. "Hell, Blinky, you don't need to worry about *me.*"

Wentworth stopped within a yard of Gabby Weismann, and looked at him very directly through the thick glasses of Blinky McQuade.

"I'm not worrying about you, Gabby," he said softly. "I'm not worrying about you at all!"

Gabby Weismann smiled weakly. He licked his thin lips, and didn't speak while Wentworth limped to the door, and closed it softly behind him. He darted across the room toward the telephone, and caught it up. He hesitated a moment, and there was a greenish cast to his face. But he finally dialed a number.

"Hello, Grogan," he said hoarsely. "This is… you-know. I got a hot tip for you. Yeah. Blinky McQuade is back in town and he's flashing about ten grand around! Slick Marshall was in on the deal, and they're at the Gotham Arms… Yeah… Yeah, I know Blinky usually works alone, but this time he teamed up. I'm telling you! That's worth fifty bucks, ain't it?"

WENTWORTH DROVE to the Gotham Arms by a roundabout route, and kept a keen eye on his back trail. He didn't trust Gabby Weismann, but he didn't give the rat credit for much sense, either. Gabby might take it into his head to follow him....

The Gotham Arms was a flash hotel, to which just such a confidence man as Slick Marshall would go when he was in the money. But no one would look askance at Blinky McQuade entering there either. The house dick would know him, of course....

Wentworth parked the coupé a half block away from the Gotham Arms, and there was a frown of concentration between his eyes. He had to work fast, for if Marshall really were tied up with Munro, it wasn't likely that Marshall would stay very long at the hotel. As he read Munro's plan, some big coup was underway which needed financing; the bank robberies which had cost a score of lives were mere preparation! Wentworth's lips twisted at the thought. Yes, the Spider had need to work fast, lest greater horror be loosed upon the people he loved!

Wentworth limped into the side entrance of Gotham Arms and let his eyes slant over the lobby. He didn't see anyone who looked dangerous to him, and he slid into a booth and used a house phone.

"What number, Jack Marshall?" he asked hoarsely.

The operator gave it to him, and Wentworth clacked up the receiver and angled toward the elevator doors. He wasn't carrying a gun. He never did, as Blinky McQuade, unless there were real danger in the immediate future. It wasn't safe for a known crook to pack a gun, lest he be picked up by the police and sent up for a long term under the Sullivan Law. But he didn't think he would need a gun to take care of Marshall. The con man wasn't a gun carrier either.

Wentworth was within a yard of the elevator when he saw a broad-shouldered figure moving toward him, and glanced around quickly to see a big man with a birthmark on his face stepping up behind him.

"Hello, Blinky," the man said easily. "It's been a long time since you paid us a visit!"

Sharp apprehension stabbed Wentworth. He knew Detective Grogan well enough, and his appearance here at this time was a little too fortuitous to be coincidence. But Blinky McQuade had committed no crimes.

"Shove off, Grogan," Wentworth snarled in Blinky's cantankerous way. "I don't like the smell of cops!"

Grogan's smile was easy on his mouth, though his eyes had a hard and wary light. "Now, that's no way to talk to a friend, Blinky," he said. "I can't understand the commissioner's choice of talking mates, but he said he'd like a little chat with you!"

Wentworth swore harshly and with feeling. "Listen, Grogan, you got nothing on me! Just because I did time once...."

Grogan stepped close, and abruptly pulled Wentworth's body hard against his for a rapid search. Wentworth's muscles jerked taut. It would have been easy to knock out Grogan then, and take to his heels, but it was damnably important now that there should be no general alarm out for him as Blinky. Also, he couldn't afford to spend the time to be taken to headquarters. There was no telling what Kirkpatrick wanted. He might even suspect that Blinky McQuade was the Spider! But there was no proof. He had committed no crime....

"Look, Grogan," he whispered hoarsely. "I'll go along all right, but—"

"I'll say you will!" Grogan growled.

"Look," Wentworth put a whine in his voice. "Look, I got a cache in the room upstairs, and I ain't trusting nobody in this dump. You know how it is!"

"A cache, hunh?" Grogan's eyes were sharp and interested.

Wentworth nodded his head rapidly. He said, bitterly, "I don't trust the cops at headquarters no more than I do the punks here, but look... there's ten grand in this roll I got cached. I don't care if you take care of it, you should peel off a grand. That's fair, ain't it? Only, I don't dare leave it in this dump, see?"

Grogan shot a glance around. "Ten grand, huh?"

Wentworth nodded. "That's right. Look, you don't need to be afraid I'll skip. There ain't nothing but empty space under the window, and it's on the twenty-second floor!"

Grogan knotted a fist into his collar, shoved him into the elevator. "Okay, punk," he said. "Twenty-second floor!"

THE OPERATOR threw the lever, turned around once to look without particular interest at Wentworth and Grogan, and after that kept his eyes on the wall sliding down past the cage door. Wentworth was thinking swiftly. He had to keep Grogan out of Marshall's room, while he made sure Marshall would wait until Blinky McQuade was released. Wentworth didn't think it would be hard for him to persuade Marshall!

He twisted against the grip on his collar. "Look, Grogan," he whispered. "You don't have to go in, do you? Look, I use this room a lot, and I got this cache...."

Grogan shook him into silence until they were on the twenty-second floor, then he let him go and Wentworth slid a hand inside his vest to the lock-pick in a vertical pocket there. He held the slim hook of surgical steel palmed in his hand.

"Look, Grogan," he said hoarsely. "I can't get away, see? Why not give me a break? Look, you can peel off a grand and a half!"

Grogan grunted, "Listen, Blinky, do I look like I ain't growed up yet?"

Blinky checked before the door, and his voice was still a whisper. Looking back at Grogan over his shoulder, he manipulated the lock-pick without a sound.

"Be a sport, Grogan," he whispered. "Hell, I can't get away, can I? On the twenty-second floor?"

There was doubt in Grogan's face, but he was a full yard behind Wentworth; and the latter now felt the lock yield under the pick. Without waiting for more, he pushed open the door, jumped inside, and in a lightning-like movement, slammed and bolted the door! On the bed, a man reared up. His hand snaked under the pillow, but Wentworth wheeled toward him, motioned silence.

"Look, it's worth a grand to me," he whispered, and snaked out his roll of bills, "to have you phone my mouthpiece, Marshall!"

Marshall swore softly, "What the hell, Blinky?" he demanded.

"Cop outside there!" Wentworth whispered.

Grogan was knocking on the
door persistently, but he wasn't
making much noise about it.
Wentworth was within a yard
of the bed now.

"Cop picked me up in the lobby," he said rapidly, "and I told
him this was my room. Knew you were here, and—"

"You had a nerve, you lousy rat!" Marshall snarled, but his
hand came out from under the pillow.

Wentworth leaped, and his fist crashed savagely against
Marshall's jaw. The man's legs kicked, and he flopped back-
ward on the bed, cold. In a single swift heave, Wentworth had
Marshall off the bed and was dragging him toward the closet.

"Just a minute, Grogan!" he called over his shoulder, placat-
ingly.

In the closet, he rapidly bound Marshall's hands and feet,
wedged a gag between his teeth. He crouched and made a rapid
search of the man's clothing. There was nothing betraying in
the clothes, except for nearly a thousand dollars in bills. From
the breast pocked of the man's coat, Wentworth fingered out a
long strip of paper. He frowned down at a railroad ticket of the
type handed out by the conductor when a cash fare paid on the
train. It was punched for Ozone Springs station, and the date
was for the day before.

WENTWORTH FROWNED over it, but there was no
time to delay. He thrust the ticket back into Marshall's pocket,

tossed his gun into the closet beside him, and sprang toward the dresser, shoved it askew from the wall, then raced to the door. He unbolted it, and the drive of Grogan's shoulder sent him reeling against the bed. Deliberately, Wentworth loosened his grip on the money, and the bills fluttered to the floor.

Grogan's questioning gaze fastened on the money greedily, and Wentworth began to talk rapidly, wheedlingly. "See, I didn't try to run out on you, Grogan. I just didn't want to give away my cache."

Grogan glanced at the dresser, grinned slyly with his fat lips. "Okay, punk. Get your money, and come on," he ordered. "But that little trick is going to cost you two grand, instead of one!"

Wentworth whined out a curse, but he didn't protest. And he submitted to the handcuffs Grogan held out. This was a bad break, but thanks to Grogan's cupidity, it need not be disastrous. Marshall would stay put until Wentworth came for him. It had never occurred to Grogan to suspect a timorous, cantankerous crook like Blinky McQuade would be committing assault behind that locked door!

At police headquarters, Grogan found that Kirkpatrick was busy and wouldn't see Blinky McQuade until the other suspects had been picked up, so Wentworth was thrust into a cell to wait. The hours dragged past; no word came to him, nor was there any hint of the purpose for which he had been taken. It took the full exertion of his mighty will to force himself to remain carelessly inactive in the cell. No man save Wentworth could, under these circumstances, have forced himself to relax in sleep!

It was the middle of the night when finally the police came

to the cell where Wentworth, his sleeping long finished, lay waiting upon his cot. Grogan was out of sorts, snarling, and he thrust Wentworth roughly before him along the cell-lined alley.

Other detectives were hazing along men Wentworth knew, and his bewilderment deepened. Con men, racketeers, a yegg who worked usually out of Chicago, were being thrust along the corridors with a half dozen others whom Wentworth did not recognize. But in a few minutes, Wentworth knew where they were heading… It was toward the lineup room!

The brightly lighted stage, the dim blur of faces beyond the bright lights that focused there, were all familiar to Wentworth. It was Kirkpatrick's voice that called from the darkness.

"We'll take Blinky McQuade first!"

Grogan grunted with satisfaction, and thrust Wentworth forward. He reached to a chair set beside the stage, picked up a dark bundle.

"Here," he ordered roughly. "Put these on, and then get up on the stage!"

Wentworth took the bundle, and the clothing drooped from his hands. He stared at it, and felt coldness race along his spine. They had given him… the cape and black hat of the Spider!

CHAPTER 9
McQUADE—FOR MURDER!

IN A single instant, the background of the entire affair flashed before Wentworth's keen brain. The Gotham Hounds were out there before the light, waiting to identify the

Spider. For what reason he and the others had been chosen as suspects, Wentworth did not know. But the comparison would be deadly to himself!

His disguise as Blinky McQuade was sound, but the personality had been deliberately designed so that, with the least possible change, he would become the Spider. Blinky McQuade walked with a limp, with hunched shoulders, even as the Spider did. If he altered his walk, the detectives would know it. If he failed to, he would be identified!

Wentworth whipped the garments high into the air and whirled toward the other men in the line. "You see it, don't you?" he howled. "They're going to frame one of us as the Spider! He's one of their pals, and they got to clear him, so we take the rap! You won't frame me, damn you! You won't frame me for the Spider!"

He flung the cloak and hat of the Spider out into the darkness, made a wild break. He wasn't actually trying to escape. That would be too suspicious, but if he could stir the others to revolt… The shouts that broke out from the file of men behind him was all that he could have hoped for. In a space of seconds, the entire line of captives was rioting.

"You ain't going to frame us into the Spider's rap!" they cried.

Grogan was after Wentworth in the darkness. A blackjack swung from his wrist, and his face was hot and angry. Wentworth whirled to confront him, dove in under the blackjack and set his arms about Grogan's body, ground his head under the man's chin.

"You slug me, Grogan!" he whispered, "and so help me God, I'll swear you took a bribe. You still got my two grand on you!"

Grogan swore angrily, but he stopped trying to use the black-jack. "You can't get away with this, Blinky!" he gasped. "Starting a riot!"

Wentworth broke away from him and sprang up on the stage in the spotlight. He shook his fists at the darkness.

"You're out there, Kirkpatrick!" he howled hoarsely. "I heard you! You aren't going to frame us for no Spider rap! You want to see the Spider, you get your pal, Wentworth, up here on the stage!"

Kirkpatrick's voice came crisply out of the darkness. "That will do, McQuade! You men, cut the fighting, or I'll send you up for a year! Understand! There won't be any parade. There doesn't need to be. We've got the man we want! Grogan, bring McQuade to my office! The rest can be released!"

On the stage, Wentworth's manner changed abruptly. He was no longer belligerent and challenging. His shoulders cringed, and his voice became a whine. "Hell, now, Commissioner," he said, "you ain't going to frame me for no rap like that! Look, I ain't done nothing, have I except stand up for my rights? You ain't got no...."

Grogan came striding out onto the stage. "Shut up, Blinky!" he snarled. "And come along!"

Wentworth winced at the big detective's approach, shivering. His mind combed frantically over what he had done, over the things he had said. There was nothing in any of it to give him away. Blinky had been built up as a pretty smart crook; smart enough to scent a frame-up in an attempt to make him parade in the Spider's clothing. But if he were wrong, he would have to make a break for it. He had wanted desperately to preserve the identity of Blinky McQuade. It was essential to him in his present course of action against Munro. And if Blinky McQuade became identified as the Spider....

His cringing accomplished its purpose. Grogan made no attempt to handcuff him but knotted his fist into Wentworth's collar and shoved him along toward Kirkpatrick's office. He was belligerent, and took every chance to grind his knuckles into Wentworth's neck, to kick his ankles and administer other petty penalties.

"Threaten me, will you!" he growled. "You lowdown rat!"

HE FAIRLY hurled Wentworth into Kirkpatrick's office, where the commissioner sat behind his desk; where Laird and Warring and Hunter sat in characteristic poses against the wall. All their eyes centered on him, but Wentworth felt reasonably secure in his disguise.

"Take off those glasses!" Kirkpatrick ordered.

Wentworth fumbled them off slowly, and managed to poke his finger into his eyes when he did it. Kirkpatrick was shrewd. He knew that the eyes were hardest of all to disguise; that such glasses as he wore would mask them completely. Uncovered, thanks to the minor injury he inflicted, Wentworth's eyes were watery and red. He blinked, squinting against the light, cringing.

"I ain't the Spider, Commissioner," he whined. "Gees, he's a flash guy. You ain't thinking...."

"Shut up," Kirkpatrick said grimly. "Walk over to the right and back again."

Warring drawled from where he rested on his spine in an arm chair, "His eyes are watering because he stuck his finger in them, taking off his glasses. I've got a pretty good ear, and I'd say his voice tones were pretty close to those of the Spider, especially when he's shouting. It's hard to alter tones in a shout."

Wentworth made no answer, but grimly he chalked up a mark for Warring. The man was smarter than he had credited. He would have to be clever indeed to escape without identification.

"Say, mister," he whined at Warring, "What are you picking on me for? I ain't never done anything to you, have I? I'm an ex-con, sure, but that ain't no reason to push me around. I want my mouthpiece!"

He was over near the printer machines which brought to Kirkpatrick news of all the precincts. On all of them simultaneously, a bell began to ring. Kirkpatrick jerked to his feet.

"Munro again!" he rasped, and strode past Wentworth toward the machine.

"Maybe not," Laird said crisply. "It's more likely they've found something in this round-up that Wentworth's friend, Miss van Sloan, recommended. It sounded very shrewd to me."

Wentworth was peering furtively toward the machine. "What's it say?" he whined. "Me cheaters... Look, can I put my glasses on?"

No one heeded him, but Grogan's eyes were focused on him watchfully. Wentworth could read the message easily. It started: *"HOMICIDE...."*

A sudden premonition raced through him. Nita had followed his orders and had reported his deductions concerning Munro's next move; they would be searching for flashy dressers, for smooth confidence men... like Slick Marshall! But he had not killed Marshall, of course. He was probably all wrong.

The bell was still clanging, while the flying keys punched out the message in deliberate rhythm. The words came out slowly, with a maddening patience....

"Man, bound and gagged, murdered in Gotham Arms."

Wentworth smothered an oath. There was no longer any doubt that it was Marshall who had been murdered; and another doubt was resolved. If Marshall had been killed, it was because he was an assistant to Munro! Nothing else made any sense. Munro had come for Marshall, found him bound and gagged. That meant, of course, that Marshall had been suspected... and Munro kept himself safe by never taking chances on a thing like that. Munro, and no one else, had killed Marshall!

Wentworth thought swiftly. His eyes searched the room, under his false brows. Kirkpatrick exclaimed something about the Gotham Arms, and Grogan moved closer to the machines. His eyes were bright and hard on Wentworth, but Wentworth scarcely heeded him. This murder meant more than that. Marshall would have told Munro who had bound him up—and henceforth Munro would know that Blinky McQuade was not what he seemed; might even come to suspect that he was the Spider!

THAT WOULD have to wait. There was a more immediate danger. Within a matter of moments, the room number would

118

come over the wire, and when it was stated, Grogan would know past any doubt that Wentworth had tricked him; he would be in a position to accuse Wentworth of murder! Either way, the value of the Blinky McQuade masquerade was finished for all time!

With the thought, Wentworth was in action!

A lithe spring put Kirkpatrick between himself and Grogan, and his hands clamped solidly on Kirkpatrick's neck. As he whipped the commissioner across the room, he snaked out the long-barreled thirty-eight that Kirkpatrick carried in a shoulder holster, and leaped for the door!

So swift had his attack been that Kirkpatrick was still reeling across the room when Wentworth reached the door and pivoted with the long-barreled revolver swaying like a snake's head in his fist.

"Everybody stand just like that," he ordered, with cold venom, "or I'll burn holes through your guts! Grogan, I'd like a chance to drop you! Don't tempt me!"

The three Hounds were grouped against the machines, and Kirkpatrick was against the outer wall of the building. Grogan was nearest to Wentworth, his face drained of color. Menace was cold in Wentworth's voice.

"Grogan will tell you," Wentworth said, "that he arrested me coming out of the room where Slick Marshall was found murdered. That's true, but I didn't bump off Marshall. Only, it ain't convenient I should stick around just now! And I ain't being framed for no Spider rap, either. Get me? *Kirkpatrick, I warned you not to move!*"

Kirkpatrick had pulled his shoulders loose from the wall.

There was a cold fire in his blue eyes, and his mouth corners were pulled down.

"You won't shoot, Blinky," Kirkpatrick said calmly, and took a step forward. "I know you now. You're the Spider, and the Spider doesn't shoot the police! You don't stand a chance, Blinky! Give yourself up! If you shoot, the whole force will be on your neck!"

Wentworth's gun was centered on Kirkpatrick and a smile tugged at his mouth corners. In that moment, he loved Kirkpatrick more than ever before. The man had the indomitable courage of a veteran soldier.

Deliberately, he squeezed the trigger of the long-barreled revolver, and Kirkpatrick's coat jerked under his left arm. Grogan started forward, and the barrel of the gun swung toward him. He checked.

"You see, Commissioner," Wentworth whispered, still in Blinky's harsh voice. "I mean business! I'll tell you one thing, and then I'm going out of here, and nobody follows... or he dies! Marshall was mixed up in that bank knock-over downtown today. Better check up on where he's been spending his time the last few days."

Alarm bells were jangling in the corridors. Wentworth could hear the shouts of running men. Kirkpatrick was smiling grimly, and he took another slow step forward.

"You've just confirmed my guess, Spider," he said. "Grogan, take him!"

At same instant he spoke, Kirkpatrick hurled himself forward. The habit of years of obedience made Grogan start forward to the attack at the same moment, Wentworth saw Laird snake a hand to an armpit gun....

Wentworth seemed to move almost lazily. The long-barreled gun sailed through the air from his right to his left hand. His right hand flicked out at the same moment and caught the wrist of Grogan as he reached out to hit. The next instant, thrown across Wentworth's out-thrust hip, Grogan sailed through the air and collided with Kirkpatrick as he lunged across the room! They went down together and the door clapped shut behind the Spider as Laird's gun crashed out.

The frosted glass panel of the door shivered into fragments and Laird's clipped, cold voice rang out. "I'll take him!" he shouted.

He reached the door, thrust his gun-hand through the opening—and the next instant, was yanked bodily into the outer office....

IT WAS split-seconds later that the outer floor of the office opened and a wedge of blue-coats poured through. Laird stood rigidly beside the door, his hand pointing toward Kirkpatrick's shattered door.

"In there!" a voice rasped. "They're fighting!"

The police charged across the room, and Wentworth, who had been holding Laird erect from behind, lowered him gently to the floor. Then Blinky McQuade faded out through the door as the charging police collided with the rush of men headed by Kirkpatrick, trying to get out of the inner office. When that mess had straightened out, Wentworth was already in the street, fading into the darkness!

The truck and the limousine had met... and the limousine was no more!

Wentworth climbed into a taxi and ordered the driver to head north. The man twisted in his seat.

"Let's see the oughday?" he demanded.

Wentworth realized with a shock that he was without any money at all. They had taken it from him at police headquarters! But he had to get away, and fast.

He said, "Certainly!" He reached beneath his coat and presented the long-barreled revolver. "Is that adequate?" he asked softly.

The driver whipped to his wheel. "Excuse me, boss!" he gasped, and the cab surged forward.

"As a matter of fact," Wentworth said softly. "I don't have any money. But I will take your name and number from your card and send it to you presently. You may depend on that."

The driver said, frantically, "Hell, skip it!"

The cab bored northward and Wentworth flicked on the radio while his brain ranged ahead. Marshall's murder proved conclusively that he was allied with Munro, and that made the railway ticket he had carried of paramount importance. Ozone Springs was a small suburban center in Westchester, and not a place to which a man of Slick Marshall's stamp would go by choice. Therefore, it must be on business connected with Munro. And....

Wentworth chuckled softly. He had just remembered that there was a sanitarium near Ozone Springs, run by a Dr. Sabrunski, who specialized in building up overworked business-men. More an athletic camp than a real sanitarium... and perfect as a hideout for Munro! But there would be more to it than a mere hideout. It could provide the headquarters where Munro could work the plan for which he had kidnapped Maurice; for which he had enlisted the services of men like Marshall!

Now the radio whined a police call… and Wentworth recognized Kirkpatrick's own voice!

"All cars, attention!" he said crisply. "This order will take precedence over all others! Pick up Blinky McQuade for murder! McQuade has been identified as a disguise of the Spider, so use maximum precautions in taking him. Also, pick up Richard Wentworth. His bail has been canceled. All cab drivers are warned to be on the lookout for him. He is armed, without funds, and in desperate haste…."

Wentworth saw the cab driver start to turn his head, then face front rigidly. The back of his neck showed taut cords, but he spoke over his shoulder.

"You don't need to get tough with me, if you're the Spider," he said. "I like the way that guy works! Saved my bacon once. My kids, that is, that was caught in a fire!"

A slow smile twisted Wentworth's lips. His heart warmed to the man's words, but Kirkpatrick's voice was still describing Blinky McQuade. Munro would know now that Blinky McQuade and the Spider were one. Yes, this masquerade was finished… and his work of catching Munro was made a dozen times more difficult. If only the police could work with him! But there were few people who thought of the Spider as other than a clever crook; a few like this taxi driver who had been helped personally.

He spoke softly, "Yes, I am the Spider," he said. "And you

won't lose by helping me. Straight north, and then west to Central Park West. I have a car parked up there."

No question as to what he must do now. He must visit Dr. Sabrunski's sanatorium at Ozone Springs, and somehow fathom the next plan of Munro... and in the meantime, dodge eighteen thousand police!

THE MID-MORNING sun was burning down hotly on the scattered white cottages of the Oak Crest sanatorium when Wentworth tooled the old and battered coupé over the last hilltop and could look down on the fenced grounds of the place. New York City had been alive with police, and it had been only after a series of narrow escapes that he had succeeded in getting out into the country. The lack of money had not simplified matters. A small loan from the friendly cabby enabled him to purchase a used suit, get hold of fresh cartridges for Kirkpatrick's gun, and assume an inconspicuous disguise.

Tennis courts were busy behind the main building; a swimming pool had its quota of pot-bellied bathers and, on the green lawn, a group of men tossed a medicine ball disinterestedly. Wentworth nodded with a frown. Nothing there to contradict his suspicions. Munro would make sure that the externals were natural. An artist in makeup would not neglect such matters.

Wentworth swung the coupé from the road, took a pair of powerful binoculars from a compartment, and made a careful scrutiny of the grounds. Finally, he thought he had found what he sought. Remote among the trees behind the sanatorium were two cottages. A smaller fence cut them off from the balance of the grounds and there was a gray-uniformed guard at the gate! That would be the place... the ward for "mental break-down" cases, in the polite medical vernacular; actually, alcoholics would normally be cared for there. And any outcries would be attributed to the delirium of the patients!

Wentworth smiled thinly, tooled the coupé back to the main road and sped on to take the sanatorium from behind. It would be doubly difficult to invade the grounds by daylight, but he could not delay. He did not know how long he could continue to evade the police—nor how soon Munro would strike again!

He succeeded in working the coupé along a wood lane to within a half mile of the sanatorium grounds; made the rest of the way rapidly on foot. The high metal fence cut through a lane of fifty feet, where trees had been cleared away. Wentworth studied the barrier through a long minute from the undergrowth, then nodded and made up his mind. The fence might very well be wired to alarms, but there was no other way to cross unless he wanted to waste a good deal of time. He would risk the alarms!

His mind made up, Wentworth sprinted across the clearing, leaped high on the fence and, with a quick swing of his body, vaulted clear! Seconds later, he was making his way swiftly toward the guarded cabins.

So far, he heard no evidence of an alarm.

The search came sooner than even he could have expected. He was still a hundred yards from the cottage which was his goal when he spotted movement in the underbrush ahead, and crouched into the shelter of dense shrubbery. Moments later, the movement revealed itself as a gray-clad guard, with a drawn automatic in his fist!

Wentworth smiled thinly and waited in his concealment. This, he thought, was luck!

The guard came on steadily, sharp eyes stabbing about him. When he was thirty feet away, Wentworth slipped from the covert. His feet made no sound, and the man's back was turned. It was only when Wentworth was sailing through the air in his final leap that the man sensed his danger, and started to whirl. He did not complete the movement....

Five minutes later, in the uniform of the guard, Wentworth stepped casually out of the woods and marched toward the cottage!

WENTWORTH'S EYES were wary and alert. He had identified the guard as a gunman once prominent in New York rackets, and it helped to confirm his suspicions that Munro had his headquarters here! He stepped boldly up to the cottage and tried the door. It resisted his thrust, and he experimented with the guard's keys until he found the right one.

Wentworth bounded inside, gun in his fist—and six men looked up apathetically from their seats about the living room. They looked at his gun, and then their heads sagged again. Despair was potent in the air, and Wentworth cursed under his breath, for he recognized every one of these men! Each was a prominent broker from Wall Street—and the president of the stock exchange, Harvey Williston, was one of the men! Yet, the morning papers had told of a stock exchange dinner the night before, which all of these men had attended.

"Williston!" Wentworth snapped. "How long have you been here?"

Williston's head lifted heavily, and his eyes were puzzled and afraid. "How long?" he asked thickly. "You ought to know, really. I mean…."

Wentworth took a stride forward. "How long?" he snapped.

The man shook his head slowly. "A week. Five days, maybe. An age!"

Through a long minute, Wentworth stood staring at the six men grouped so apathetically about the room; remembered the guards and the extra precaution of the fence. And this despair… Wentworth could feel depression eating at his spirit, and he swore softly. No question what that meant! Munro was directing upon these captives the device by which he could control emotions.

"By God!" Wentworth cried softly. "That's it! That's Munro's plan!"

He wheeled from the room, locked the door behind him. He had to get word to New York! He strode rapidly down the path toward the gate, toward the main building of the sanitarium! The guard there looked up sharply, but recognized the uniform and looked back to the magazine he was reading. Wentworth's gaze probed toward the main building. He would have to knock out this guard, and there were a dozen windows overlooking the man.

"Hey!" he called, hoarsely. "Get up here, quick! Something damned funny!"

He turned and hurried back toward the cottage, ducked inside. The guard at the gate hesitated, then toiled after him up the slight grade. Wentworth waited for him just inside the door. His punch was clean and hard to the jaw... Afterward, he hurried again toward the sanitarium. His mind raced quickly. He couldn't afford to go through the main exchange of the building, nor could he delay to find Munro. The office of Dr. Sabrunski would probably have a direct wire at least to the village of Ozone Springs....

He passed the group of medicine ball-tossers at a distance of fifty feet, but no attention was paid to him in the gray guard's uniform. He strode in through the main entrance, saw a male nurse in a white jacket and turned the other way. His feet echoed along the hallway, and his eyes ranged ahead, picked out the door of Sabrunski's office. But he sought a private exit....

He turned the corner of the hallway, and found it. He crouched over the lock, and his fingers were sly with the lock-pick he was never without. The bolt yielded silently, and he eased open the door a slight crack. It was Sabrunski's office all right, and it was empty!

Wentworth waited only to lock the door again, then he bounded to the two telephones set upon the desk, snatched up the one that showed a number placard on its face. "Commissioner Kirkpatrick, New York City police!" he snapped "This is an emergency call!"

THE CONNECTION went through swiftly and Wentworth, waiting, drew Kirkpatrick's long revolver from his waistband and put it under his hand on the desk. His eyes were narrow on the door of the outer office, and grimness traced his jaw in knotted muscles.

"Wentworth speaking," he said curtly, when he heard Kirkpatrick speak over the wire. "Quiet for a moment, Kirk. This is overwhelmingly important! I've fathomed Munro's new plan. He has kidnapped six members of the stock exchange, including the president! They're prisoners at the Oak Crest sanitarium, Ozone Springs. *Listen!* Munro is going to rig the stock market through his emotion machine. He'll probably concentrate on the floor of the exchange and drive them crazy with fear so that prices tumble to the bottom. For God's sake, get down there and stop it before what little prosperity that there is—is destroyed!

"Yes, I'll give you the names of the six men. Williston, the president... What? Good God in heaven, then it's already started. Get down there fast, Kirk. Yes, the others are—"

The door of the office opened without warning, and a quick-moving, stoop-shouldered man with a mane of fiery red hair came striding into the room. Instantly, Wentworth snatched up the gun, and leveled it.

"Close the door and come in," Wentworth ordered quietly. *"This is the end, Munro!"*

The man stiffened. "Put down that phone, fool!" he snapped. "Don't you recognize me? I am Dr. Sabrunski!"

Wentworth smiled thinly, and his gun hand did not waver. He spoke softly, into the telephone, "Hello, Kirk, I have Munro a prisoner here!"

The phone had no vibration in it, and Wentworth's eyes contracted. He spoke into the instrument again, set it slowly into its cradle. It was not that the connection had been broken; the instrument itself was dead! Somebody, without moving after he had entered the room, Dr. Sabrunski-Munro had contrived that!

The man was smiling slowly, with a deep movement of full lips. Behind gold-rimmed spectacles, his eyes seemed benevolent, but there was nothing kindly in his voice.

"Ah, now I know you!" he said softly. "You are the Spider. It is you who created this little disturbance in the isolated cottage!"

Facing the man, Wentworth felt cold anger flow through him. This was the fiendishly clever, utterly ruthless devil who had murdered by torture so that he might line his pockets! He had him under his gun muzzle now, and there could be only one fate for him.

Munro shook his head, "No, you dare not shoot me, Wentworth, or Spider, or whatever you call yourself," he said. "You told Kirkpatrick you, as Wentworth, held me prisoner! If now, the Spider kills me… you see? You are afraid!"

Wentworth swore softly, and realized that he *was* afraid! There was nothing physical in the fear that ran through his breast. He knew that, once more without seeming to move, Munro had contrived to focus a fear-creating machine upon him! But that knowledge did not allay the rising tide of dread and apprehension that crept through him. He brought his powerful will to bear to combat the terror. His mouth became a compressed slit.

"Yes, I am afraid," he said slowly, "through your damnable machine. *But it will not save your life!*"

Wentworth slowly lifted the heavy revolver, and resolution was as iron in his soul! Nothing mattered now, save the destruction of Munro! He lifted the revolver and saw, with unutterable dismay, that his hand was shaking! The hand of the Spider that never trembled under any assault of horror or despair, was shaking like the hand of a foolish child!

Munro's smile had become sardonic. "You are terror-stricken!" he said amiably. "No matter how hard you try, you cannot even pull the trigger of that gun!"

SLOWLY, WENTWORTH eased himself down into the chair behind the desk. He braced his forearm on the desk, and deliberately set about Munro's execution! In spite of the support of the desk, Wentworth's hand still shook badly. He could not be sure of his aim, even at this short range of twenty feet!

"You cannot even pull the trigger!" Munro whispered.

Wentworth strained at the trigger and could not budge it! The perspiration sprung out on his forehead. Deliberately, Wentworth contracted all the muscles of his body! He started with his right leg, and drew the tension up through his thigh, along his side and into his shoulder. His hand was shaking erratically, but Munro dared not move toward him, lest the slightest movement shake the power he and his machine exerted. The contraction crept along Wentworth's right arm, as the will of the Master of Men drove it on, slowly.

He knew that his first shot would miss. It could not help but miss with his hand shaking so wildly. But he thought the shot would snap the paralysis through sheer shock, and after that....

Wentworth felt the tension slide into his hand, saw the cording of his tendons in titanic effort. Ah! His trigger finger....

The blast of the gun was like a cannon, and Munro went backward, reeling. His hand slashed out against the wall, even as Wentworth ripped the muzzle of the gun around… and the floor went out from beneath Wentworth!

His fall was as sudden as death, but there was no jar. The chair merely slid down a steep, smooth incline and rocketed out across another room below Munro's office. It brought to a halt against an overstuffed davenport, and Wentworth was instantly out of the chair, leaping for the incline. He knew that Munro, in desperation, had dropped him down an escape chute that had been intended for Munro himself in extremity.

Wentworth was scrambling up the slide, gun ready in his fist, when the trapdoor in the floor slapped shut! In the same instant, alarm bells began to clang throughout the building!

Wentworth wasted no more time in futile efforts to burst through the trapdoor. Munro was already in full flight, but there was one thing he would contrive to do before he fled. He would kill those six captives!

Wentworth knew that without thought. It was Munro's technique, to leave no one who might be a witness against him! Wentworth hurled himself at the door of the room, whipped it open and savage gunfire blazed at him from the darkness of the outer corridor, in which every light had been extinguished. Wentworth's gun bucked in his fist and he lunged aside into the protection of the darkness. But the Spider did not fire blindly. He never did. His keen eyes had spotted each spot that blossomed fire, and one of his slugs sped toward each flame!

Wentworth fired three shots, and through the rolling echoes of his blasting, silence fell suddenly upon the corridor. One man was running away, but the other two made no sounds at all.

Grimly, Wentworth flung himself forward in a headlong sprint in the wake of the man who fled. He was in a central, basement corridor of the building, but he was speeding in the direction he wished to go—toward the cottage on the slope of the hill! The screams of the fleeing man cut off behind the closing of a door, and Wentworth raced past it, on toward the end of the corridor. There was another door there, and Wentworth fired twice as he darted toward it, took off in a leap that drove his entire weight, shoulder-first, against the barrier.

It crashed open, and Wentworth plunged through, reeling. A window... Wentworth scooped up a chair and sent it hurtling before him. The glass exploded outward and, before the fragments had shivered to the earth, which was level with the sill, Wentworth was through the opening.

AHEAD OF him lay the graceful slope of the sanatorium lawn, the fence and the cottage. A man was going through that gate this very instant, a man with a mane of fiery red hair. Wentworth flung up the revolver, realized that Munro was out of range and began once more to sprint. He could feel the hard pounding of his heart, keeping pace to the thud of his feet on the soft turf. A clear exultation was in his soul. This was victory!

He darted through the gate, and the door of the cottage was closed! Wentworth's eyes stabbed beyond, but the woods yielded no trace of Munro... and then, within the cottage, a man screamed!

A shout rose to Wentworth's throat, and he took the slope in two-yard leaps. The glass in the door shivered as the whole barrier crashed in under the drive of his shoulder. He staggered through the opening, and there was a muffled blast in the adjoining room! From the fireplace, tongues of flame starred out into the room, driving before them coiling, greasy green spirals and puffs of Munro's torture gas!

Wentworth's gun vibrated in his fist, and the glass smashed out of the windows in the room.

"Out the windows!" he shouted at the stunned men. "Out the windows, before I kill you!"

He sent a bullet slapping into the back of the davenport beside Williston's shoulder, and the man yelped and leaped to his feet. He plunged out the window and Wentworth flung more lead close to the others, jarred them into motion.

In the nick of time, Wentworth sprang backward out of the doorway. The greedy tentacles of the green gas crawled after him, and he leaped on to the ground. Five of the men were picking themselves up from the earth, but the sixth had begun to scream. He was clawing at his face, with futile, frantic hands! Even as Wentworth raced forward in a hopeless effort to help him, the man reeled to his feet and began to run. His face was a fleshless skull!

Wentworth sprang toward the other five men. "Get up the hill!" he ordered. "Toward the fence! And hurry!"

The roaring blast of a motor startled him and he whipped about. From a shadow that seemed only a fold in the hill, but obviously hid the mouth to an underground garage, a powerful car leaped out. As it rolled down the slope, a machine gun began to spit from its window. The slugs tore up the earth under Wentworth's feet, glanced whining into the air. They rattled among the tree branches and another of the fleeing men screamed, and fell threshing to the earth. He continued to scream with every breath.

Wentworth flung prone and whipped up the revolver, but he knew, subconsciously, that he had only one shot left though he had reloaded in that swift pursuit across the lawn of the sanitarium. Desperately, he squeezed off the shot, saw the car lurch as the bullet took effect on a tire. It lurched, reeled, and dashed on!

Wentworth staggered to his feet, but the car was sweeping about to bring the machine gun into line again. Wentworth turned and dashed on toward the four men who remained on their feet. They still stared stupidly at the trees about them, at the man who kept screaming… They were still dazed from their long captivity under the dominance of Munro's emotion-machine! Wentworth hurled curses at them, drove them into the shelter of the trees. He fumbled more cartridges from his pockets, stuffed the chambers of his revolver… suddenly realized that the drone of the automobile motor was diminishing.

HE WHIRLED about, peered through the trees, and saw the car whip around behind the sanatorium. Moments later, there was the roar of another powerful engine. An airplane! It ripped into sight from behind the building, skated into the air with only yards to spare above the fence, soared toward the sky. Then it whirled back toward the woods!

Wentworth swore in despair. Against the machine gunning of an airplane, he was helpless, though the trees would furnish some cover. He herded the four men together and drove them away from the fence, through the woods to eastward. The airplane motor whined up to high pitch, and slugs began to rip through the trees behind them. But this once Munro had miscalculated. He had thought Wentworth would make straight for the fence.

Presently, the plane roared off in a bee-line for New York City, and Wentworth could get the weary men over the fence and race toward his coupé. He dragged Williston into the machine, told the others how to reach the main road, and jammed on the gas. The remaining three men would be safe enough now. Munro was the leader, and without him, the killers would think only of flight. Yes, they would be safe… but the stock market in New York was going crazy! Men were being stripped of their fortunes through the machinations of Munro!

Wentworth bore the accelerator to the floor and the powerful engine beneath that battered hood hummed its song of might. Wentworth was racing not alone to save the fortunes of the men on the exchange, though the crash of the market might bring the renewing prosperity of America tumbling about the ears of the multitudes. But Munro would be there. No doubt as to where he was headed. And Munro must be destroyed, lest scores, and hundreds more die under the torture of that awful gas, under the torment of the machine that could drive men mad with terror!

At the first town, Wentworth dragged his racing car to a halt, and bolted into a store to find a telephone. He slammed through another call to Kirkpatrick. It was possible that, by intercepting the plane, the police could seize Munro before he could do any further harm!

His phone call went through swiftly, but it was not Kirkpatrick who answered the phone. It was Captain Fillarty.

"The Commissioner went down to the exchange an hour ago," Fillarty said, and worry was in his voice. "Haven't had any orders from him that make sense, but a little while ago, he had me send a cop over to his safety deposit box to bring him all his securities! He sounded scared as hell—or just plain crazy!"

CHAPTER 10
RULE OF TERROR!

WENTWORTH PRESSED down the despair that rose to his throat. He needed no more than that to know that Kirkpatrick had succumbed to the virus of terror that Munro had loosed upon the exchange. But Wentworth could not blame him. He himself had been so terrified he could not shoot straight!

He threw his information at Fillarty, gave the license number of the plane, and rapidly put through another call for Nita. In swift words, he told her what had happened to Kirkpatrick.

"This is what you must do," he said. "Fasten a strip of some kind of metal about your head, pressing it down behind the ears. Fasten wires to that strip, and group them in plates upon the heels of your shoes. Go to the exchange then, and see if you can get Kirkpatrick outside, and insulate him the same way. You'll be safe then from the terror!"

Nita agreed without question, but threw words at him quickly before he could hang up. "Dick, Warring wasn't robbed of that camera with which he took pictures of the Spider! He hid it, to prevent its being stolen, or seized by the police! He bragged about it to me yesterday. And he'll be here in a few minutes to take me down and help him recover it! I'm going to get those pictures, Dick!"

Wentworth said, violently, "There's no time, Nita! Get to the exchange, and let the pictures wait! Nita…."

It was no use. She was gone… and he knew that she would delay help at the exchange to recover those pictures. Nor would telephoning again help matters at all. He flung back behind the wheel of the coupé and sent it racing out through the city streets, boring into the long miles to New York.

Beside him, Williston, the president of the stock exchange, was beginning to recover a little. He asked slow questions and Wentworth flung information at him. Anger began to burn in Williston's face.

"I'll fix that!" he snapped. "Just get me to a telephone!"

Wentworth shook his head. "You don't understand, Williston. You're on the stock exchange right now. That is, a man who looks and talks and behaves exactly like you, is on the stock exchange. Every one of those other five who were with you is being perfectly impersonated also! Through those five men, and your own double, Munro—you know him as Dr. Sabrunski—will be cashing in heavily on this panic. When it is over, he will cash in the other way, by buying at the bottom of the market! Our only chance is to get there in person, and face down the impostors!"

Long before Wentworth had reached the outskirts of the city, the radio he had switched on brought him the news that an airplane had crashed in Bowling Green… but without any pilot in the cockpit. Wentworth's lips drew bitterly thin. Munro had jumped out by parachute, obviously, and would be even now making his way to the stock exchange to thwart any effort to uncover his operations! Munro was on his way there… and Nita, despite her delay, should be already on the scene!

Those last miles of ripping down the West Side highway, the last half of the way with police sirens screaming in pursuit, seemed endless to Wentworth. Williston sat stiffly forward, hands braced against the cowling, and did not seem to notice that the speedometer needle wavered above a hundred miles an hour most of the way. The wind was a solid wall that yielded reluctantly, whining about the coupé. Other cars skittered frantically from their path.

The sweep down the final ramp was like a landing in a racing plane. The tires screamed as Wentworth whipped the coupé over, and sent it scuttling through the narrow canyons of the financial district toward the stock exchange. As Williston batted open the door, Wentworth lunged to the pavement. He caught sight of Nita in the corridors before the broad doors of the Floor itself, and leaning against the wall beside her, was Kirkpatrick! A strip of metal bound his temples, and wires dangled to the floor. He looked about him with the dazed incredulity of a man awaking from a nightmare.

WENTWORTH BOLTED past him, dragging Williston with him, and even so soon, Wentworth could begin to feel the crawling fear that gripped the entire building.

"Blow out the electric system!" Wentworth shouted back over his shoulder. "Pull the main switch, and be quick about it!"

Kirkpatrick shivered under the lash of his words, and Nita was running toward Wentworth.

"I got them, Dick!" she called, and shook her purse.

Wentworth nodded. "Keep off the Floor, Nita. There will be danger!"

Williston plunged through the doorway, with Wentworth a stride behind him. The Floor was a shambles. Men were going mad with fright, and it shone from their eyes. Their clothing was torn, and their voices harsh from shouting. Wentworth took a single glance at the big board with its electric lights that flashed the prices and consternation stopped him in his tracks. Even in his wildest imaginings, he had not expected such prices as these! The bottom had fallen out with a vengeance!

Williston was charging across the floor toward a man who was, in every way, a replica of himself. About this man was none of the wild disorder that marked the others. He faced about coolly as Williston dashed up. His eyes widened in surprise, then he whirled and called sharply to the guards.

"Arrest this man!" he shouted. "He is an impostor!"

Wentworth flashed past Williston and seized the poseur by the neck. His fingers tore at the flesh, found the thing he sought… two fine wires that ran down from beneath the wig that covered his head. Wentworth yanked at them savagely, and they broke.

"Now, fool!" Wentworth panted. "Now, Munro's fear machine is working on you! You are terrified! You will confess, for you are discovered!"

The man looked into Wentworth's stern face, and his own

countenance turned pale. Wentworth's whole body was braced against the fear that was consuming him, but he would not yield. He could not. He was the Master of Men! He shook the fake Williston violently by the neck.

"Confess, fool!" he cried. "Where is Munro?"

The man's lips sagged open, and from the gallery of the Floor, a shot crashed out raggedly! The jar of the bullet, striking into his prisoner's body, jerked the man from Wentworth's grasp, tumbled him to the floor, dead. Wentworth flopped flat behind him, raked out his revolver... and saw only the swinging doors of the gallery through which the killer already had disappeared.

But Wentworth needed no second guess to know the man's identity. It was Munro!

Instantly, he was on his feet and running. As he took off in a vaulting leap for the balcony railing, he heard a gong clang out peremptorily, and Williston's sharp voice cry out:

"The exchange is closed!"

So that peril was averted for the moment. By tomorrow, the explanations would be out, and confidence should be restored. The thought was a flash across his brain as his up-reaching hands snagged the railing of the gallery. He swung himself up, yanked the gun from his trouser band, and plunged in pursuit of Munro.

Yes, the exchange would be equable tomorrow, but the people had no protection against Munro. There could be only one protection, and that was Munro's death!

Wentworth flung himself out into the corridor behind the balcony, and the way was empty. The steps... Wentworth reached them in a half dozen bounds, circled downward. It was just as he skated out into the first floor hallway that he heard a woman scream—Nita!

He raced for the outer doors, and a motor roared into violent life out there. He plummeted out into the street, gun lifted in his fist. It was his own coupé that was roaring around the corner! He had just a brief glimpse of Nita's slumped body, of Munro hunched over the wheel. Before even the Spider's lightning speed could squeeze off a single shot, the car had ripped around the corner out of sight, and was gone!

WENTWORTH'S EYES quested desperately over the street for a car. There were one or two, but they would stand no chance at all of overtaking his own powerful coupé. If Kirkpatrick's car were near now! Wentworth ran for the corner, and a long, sleek limousine rolled out of the side street. The bearded Sikh behind the wheel leaned out to throw the door wide.

"I came with the *missie sahib, sahib!*" cried Ram Singh.

Wentworth sprang gratefully into the rear of his own limousine, flung a hand out to point.

"Down that side street!" he gasped. "Munro has kidnapped the *missie sahib!*"

The mighty engine of the Daimler began to roar, and the limousine surged across Broadway with a smooth burst of power, hurtled down grade toward the Hudson. West Street was empty of any sign of the fugitive coupé with its precious burden, and when the Daimler charged up the ramp of the elevated speed highway, that, too, was deserted. Wentworth was sitting tensely forward in the rear, and his keen eyes combed the way in vain.

The Daimler arrowed along the drive at mounting speed, but still there was no trace of the car they sought.

Cursing, Wentworth ordered the Sikh back to street level, as it became clear that Munro had doubled on his trail to elude them, but it was too late. Emptiness everywhere; and Munro had made good his escape!

Wentworth beat his temples with his fists. "Munro can't escape," he said thickly. "He can't. There must be a way to trace him. Ah, Maurice!"

Wentworth sat bolt upright. "That's it," he muttered. "Maurice! He is being hunted by the police in the belief that he and Munro are the same man. Yes, he would make sure that Maurice was found, dead, before he finally vanished! Now, I need only to find Maurice!"

Wentworth caught wild laughter surging into his throat, forced himself to calmness. He need only do, in a few brief hours—but probably only minutes remained!—what eighteen thousand police had been attempting for days! But perhaps Nita would find some way of signaling him? There was a two-way radio in the coupé in which she was fleeing. There was a slim chance....

Dispiritedly, Wentworth switched on the radio of the car, and words slashed out at him immediately, words in the mocking tones of Munro!

"I hope you are listening, Wentworth!" Munro said. "I am keeping Nita with me for a while. Also the things that she carries. I am sure you will understand! Presently, I will have orders for you, Wentworth, and it would be wise if you obey!

Otherwise, I'm afraid you will never see Nita alive again, even briefly!"

Wentworth was working the direction finder of the car rapidly, but he had barely begun when the radio went dead! Still, it definitely pointed uptown. Uptown, in Manhattan? But how to find one man and one woman….

Slowly, the firm line of his lips began to curve. He whipped forward. "Get me to a telephone, Ram Singh!"

Minutes later, he was bounding into a cigar store, into a phone booth. He put through a call to the Cornell Medical Center, asked for the staff physician of the psychiatric department by name.

"This is Richard Wentworth," he said rapidly. "I need some information vitally. There is in New York City somewhere, I remember having read, a small hospital which has experimented extensively in the control of mental cases with music. Can you tell me the name and address of that hospital? Yes, that's it! The Durward Memorial! Off Riverside Drive!"

WENTWORTH CLASHED up the receiver, and put through a call to police headquarters. "Fillarty? Wentworth… Munro will be found at the Durward Memorial Hospital. He has prisoners there he will murder if you storm the place. Order a quiet encirclement, and try to catch him coming out! Yes! No, I'm not issuing orders to you, Fillarty, but if it's learned you had this information and didn't act on it, then heaven help the entire police force."

Wentworth slammed up the receiver and vaulted across the walk into the Daimler, sent it hurtling northward again. His hand dropped to the left side of the cushion, pressed a hidden button there, and the seat slid slowly forward, revolved to reveal the secret wardrobe in its back. Wentworth bent tensely over the make-up tray, and the lighted mirror racked there. Long before the giant Daimler swung off the elevated highway and circled toward the hospital, Wentworth was ready. His face had changed incredibly; a beaked predatory nose, lipless mouth, the long, lank hair were those of the Spider.

The Daimler slid to a halt before the doors of the Durward Memorial, and Wentworth leaped out. "Wait around the corner!" he snapped at Ram Singh. "If Munro attempts an escape, stop him!"

In the entrance hall of the small, private hospital, Wentworth checked. He threw back his head and sent the eerie, mocking laughter pealing through the corridors!

A nurse screamed, looked into the corridor from a doorway, and then began to run up the stairs, still crying out in a hoarse, frenzied way. An elevator door popped open, and a man peered out. For an instant, the eyes of the two men met, and then Wentworth uttered a shout and whipped out his automatic! He bounded toward the door, but the man had ducked inside. The door slammed shut, and the elevator was dropping toward the basement! Wentworth darted at the steel door above which a red light burned, and the door was rigidly locked.

His gun kicked against his fist, slamming lead into the lock, but still the door resisted. Screams burst out over the buildings, and there was the sound of men running in the corridor behind him. Above the clatter, Wentworth heard the roar of an automobile engine starting up!

Wentworth whirled and raced toward the front exit again. Hospital attendants scattered before his charge like leaves before the wind. As he hit the sidewalk, there was a grinding crash of metal around the corner, a hoarse cry.

Wentworth flashed out past the corner of the building, and skated to a halt. The Daimler was a piled wreck in the middle of the street and, on the walk, Ram Singh lay motionless! His right hand gripped his knife, and there was blood spreading from beneath that arm.

Dwindling up the broad reach of Riverside Drive was a heavy, closed truck as large as a moving van!

Even as Wentworth watched, Ram Singh staggered to his feet. His right arm swung limply at his side, but curses of pure rage poured from his lips. Wentworth bolted back around the corner, his eyes seeking desperately for a car he could use... and a limousine swung to the curb. From the front seat beside the driver, a man leaped to the pavement with a gun in his fist.

"All right, Spider!" he shouted. "We've got you this time!"

Wentworth was staring into the cold, courageous eyes of Carl Laird!

THE SPIDER laughed... and the gun in his right fist streaked out flame! The gun was wrenched from Laird's hand as if by a mighty fist, and a moment later Wentworth was upon him.

"Back into the car!" the Spider's voice rasped. "Back, I say, or I'll blow you apart!"

Laird stumbled into the back of the car, and Wentworth flung himself into the front seat while Warring and Hunter were groping for their guns.

"Roll this car!" Wentworth rasped at Hunter, behind the wheel. *Roll it!* Munro is escaping!"

Hunter stepped down on the gas, and the car lurched forward, made a screaming turn into Riverside Drive. Wentworth swayed easily to the rocking of the machine, and his two guns were restless. One rested against Hunter's side, and the other covered the two men in the rear seat. Warring, he saw, was smiling as usual.

"Laird," Wentworth ordered softly, "you will reach over with your left hand and take the gun from Warring's coat pocket. You will throw it out the door!"

Laird obeyed with stiff movements. His right hand hung limply at his side, and there was a trace of blood on the fingers from lead that had spattered from Wentworth's bullet. At Wentworth's further orders, he picked up two pairs of handcuffs from the floor, fastened his left wrist to Warring's right, with the link over the coat-rail that ran across the back of the front seat. Wentworth turned his attention then to Hunter, disarmed him, and handcuffed him to the wheel.

"I regret these inconveniences, gentlemen," Wentworth said mockingly, in the Spider's flat voice, "but certain injustices are sometimes necessary in the pursuit of justice outside the law! I take it you were at police headquarters when Wentworth phoned in that report? Yes I'm afraid we'll find the poor devil is in that truck ahead, with Nita, and a peculiarly vicious killer named Munro. You are going to overtake him, Hunter!"

Hunter nodded stiffly. His face was very pale, but his hands were firm on the steering wheel, and his foot bore heavily on the accelerator.

Laird said gravely, "I underestimated you, Spider!"

Wentworth did not answer him. His eyes were boring ahead on the truck. It heeled heavily and swung into the ramp that stretched up toward the George Washington Bridge!

Wentworth's eyes leaped ahead to the magnificent stretch of the bridge, two hundred feet above the river, and his lips were pale. In God's name, what did Munro plan? A quiver ran through his body, and he felt the sudden slowing of the car. He whipped toward Hunter, and the man's face was completely drained of color, his eyes wide in… in *terror!*

Wentworth swore and jammed his foot down on top of Hunter's, bearing the accelerator to the floor.

"Steer, damn you!" Wentworth rasped, "or you'll be killed!"

A whimpering moan came to Hunter's lips, but he clung desperately to the steering wheel. Wentworth twisted about, and even Laird showed fear upon his face.

"Don't be fools!" Wentworth said, and his voice was strained. "You understand what's happening, don't you? That devil, Munro, has got his fear-generating apparatus in that truck ahead. It's working on us now. That's all it is!"

Hunter gasped, "I'm *afraid!*"

Wentworth had to force out words against the shaking of his whole body. "There's nothing to be afraid of," he said hoarsely. "Listen, I'll tell you how Munro generates fear, and then you'll understand that there's nothing to fear."

THERE WERE cars in the other lane of the driveway, heading downhill in the opposite direction. Things seemed to go wrong in that line of traffic as the great racing truck blundered past. Men lost their nerve, and with it the control of the cars. Horns blared wildly, as if the autos themselves were screaming. There was a frantic scream, and a car wrenched broadside in the stream of traffic. In a second, four other cars had smashed into it. They veered together toward the stone balustrade, and it did not hold them.

"Nothing to be afraid of," Wentworth repeated hoarsely. "In that hospital, they experimented with the control of mental cases through musical rhythms. With the use of that great, evil mind of his, Munro found out what those rhythms were. He analyzed the rhythms that are accidents in music, bringing a little lightness of heart sometimes; at others, grief, or even fear. By winnowing out those basic rhythms and emphasizing them to the exclusion of everything else, he found out how to play upon the emotion of men, especially men in the mass where the mob spirit can take hold of them!"

Laird was trying fiercely to concentrate. "I have heard nothing!" he said harshly. "I can hear nothing now!"

Wentworth shook his head. "That's the hellish part of it," he said. "If people understood, they might fear less. He has converted those sounds into electric impulses which play directly upon the brain itself! That is all it is. That's what makes us afraid now, the beating of unseen waves upon our brains. The rhythms of music. Is that a thing to fear?"

Laird said, "No, but I'm afraid!"

Wentworth laughed wildly. "I'm not afraid!" he cried. "We can not be afraid. We must not be afraid!"

The car was screaming into the last wild turn toward the bridge. Hunter was clinging desperately to the wheel. His foot struggled to be free from the grip of Wentworth's, on the accelerator, but could not.

But the truck was rolling again, gathering momentum and speed. Wentworth struck the glass of the window beside him and drove it out. He leaned his body out of the window, and began to shoot. His automatic rose and fell as steadily as on the target range. Two shots, and the two tires on the right rear of the truck went out with a hissing blast.

The truck veered wildly, rocking and swaying… but losing speed! It swung crazily to the right, toward the guard rail.

Desperately, Wentworth squeezed off two more shots and the two left rear tires of the truck exploded under the impact of his lead. The truck straightened out, but the tires began to dance and wobble crazily. The truck was barely crawling, but it was squarely in the middle of the roadway, so wide that it could not be passed. Abruptly, the truck jerked to a halt!

With a great cry, Wentworth wrenched on the handbrake of the car, and ripped the ignition key from the lock.

"You'll stay as witnesses!" he cried back over his shoulder, as he raced toward the truck. He saw the cab door bounce open, and flung two bullets against it as he bounded forward at top speed. The door slammed shut, and Wentworth heard a scream; heard Nita scream! At the same moment, he realized the truck was rolling backward!

A hoarse cry lifted into Wentworth's throat. He saw legs on the other side of the truck. Munro had leaped to the ground with Nita... but the truck was rolling backward! And the car, with the three Gotham Hounds helpless prisoners within it, was fairly in the truck's path!

Wentworth's guns lifted. He heard Nita cry out again, in pain... He had no target. With a despairing cry, Wentworth whirled and began to race down the gradient toward the stationary car. He could see Laird and the rest fighting desperately against the handcuffs, but that was futile.

Back there, Nita was being carried off by Munro, but Wentworth could not condemn these three men to the horrible death that was rolling toward them.

THE SCREAMS of the three men came to him now, even above the pound of his feet, above the rumble of the truck. He dared a glance over his shoulder. He was twenty-five feet ahead of the juggernaut, but now it was rolling almost as swiftly as he could run! There would be no time to use keys on those handcuffs.

Wentworth hit the running board beside Hunter in a flying leap. He reached through the window with both hands and seized the steering wheel. With all the power of his mighty muscles, the incredible concentration of his force and will together, he heaved on that steering wheel... and it snapped. It came free from its cross-bars, and Wentworth tumbled to the roadway. He was up in an instant, and Hunter was fumbling his way out of the door. Wentworth had his gun in his hand and, as he flung toward the car again, he began shooting.

153

Twice more, as he leaped toward the car, Wentworth flung his bullets and they slashed into the upholstery at one end of the bar to which the two men were cuffed.

"Pull!" Wentworth shouted.

Laird and Warring looked at him, and their lips moved with words that Wentworth could not hear; could not even listen to. He reached in through the window once more, set his mighty shoulders.

Wentworth hit the pavement on his shoulders, and Warring catapulted out on top of him, dragging Laird by the handcuffs on their wrists. Instantly, Wentworth was rolling, thrusting them away from himself toward the side of the roadway. Hunter was out there, screaming, jumping up and down. The rumble of the truck was overbearing, was on top of them.

Frantically, Wentworth thrust Laird and Warring before him, heard the roar of the truck on top of him, and felt crushing weight on his shoulders. It increased intolerably. Cloth tore. Wentworth's eyes, straining upward, saw the body of the truck towering above him... then the strain released. With a final desperate lunge, he hurled his body against those of Laird and Warring, driving them inches to safety.

Wentworth staggered to his feet, reeling backward from the concussion that beat upon him. The truck and the limousine had met... and the limousine was no more!

Wentworth looked down at himself, and saw that the tire of the truck had squeezed past his shoulder with the fraction of an inch to spare. It had been the pinching of the pressure on his clothes that had compressed him. He staggered when he stooped to catch up his gun. He was reeling when he began to run once more along the bridge toward where he had last seen Nita and Munro. His eyes quested wildly over an empty roadway, swept to the sidewalk… and a cry that was almost a scream mounted into his throat!

Nita was fighting desperately, but Munro held her helpless from behind, and even as Wentworth watched, Munro mounted to the railing of the bridge!

For the first time, Wentworth became aware of the other people on the bridge. They were stampeding in wild terror, in the madness that Munro's damnable machine brought on. Munro clung to the cable with the hand that gripped his gun, and the other arm was wrapped about Nita. He began to shoot….

WENTWORTH WAS sprinting desperately. He was no more than fifty feet away, but he might as well have been fifty miles. He stood no chance at all to save Nita… and Munro! He could not even shoot at the author of all this horror!

But Wentworth's lips were set in a rock-firm line and his swift brain was working. As he ran, he thrust his guns back into their holsters, and snaked out the silken Web! No time to uncoil it. Wentworth grasped an end, and threw the coil from him violently, threw it high toward an overhead cable that arched down from the sky. He was running, and the coil sailed high. It crossed the cable and swung back toward him. Wentworth was already in the air.

Munro's face was twisted into a mask of hatred and fury. As Wentworth swept toward him, he struck at Nita's hand with the butt of the gun, and pushed her body away from him, tried to plunge her to death in the waters far below!

Wentworth had ripped his gun from its holster now. Too late to thrust it back. Too late to do anything at all, except to pray speed into the swing toward the railing where Nita's sweet body was toppling toward death. He was only ten feet away and traveling with the speed of the wind, and he seemed to float tantalizingly. The flapping of the cape, stiffened straight out from his shoulders, was a brake upon his movement. His left hand, twisted and knotted into the rope, was aching with the grip. He… swung out over the rail!

Sweeping downward with his free arm, Wentworth flung it around Nita's body just below the shoulders, scooped her up against his chest. The strain on his left hand lifted a cry of sheer agony to his throat. Bones were breaking there, but it was knotted too tightly to let go. He was sweeping out, out over space. Far below were the steely waters.

Wentworth twisted his head about, uttered a cry of horror and despair. Munro was still poised on the railing, but he had discarded the revolver. Instead, he grasped in his hand something that glinted evilly in the rays of the slanting sun, evil and green glistening; a bomb of the flesh-eating gas!

It was only then that Wentworth remembered he had his automatic in the fist that was knotted under Nita's arm. But he could not point it. He could not free Nita to point the gun. He strained Nita closer against his breast while he twirled there at the end of the rope.

The jar of the gun in his knotted fist almost shook loose his grip upon Nita. He shut his jaw hard and shot again, again. Munro's mocking laughter came to him; mocking and triumphant. Fiercely, Wentworth jerked up his arm, bringing Nita with it, lifting her face to his... and once more pulled the trigger.

The gun tore loose from his fingers. A cry lifted to his throat and, for that first instant, he thought that it was he who had screamed. But no such cry as that ever came from the Spider's lips. Why... why, good God, it was Munro!

THEY SWUNG past the railing of the bridge again, and Munro was there. His out-thrust right hand was alive with the burning cold green fires of the gas, and he was screaming as he leaned out from the railing. He was pitching out into space. His scream came up, up, for an incredible while, faded out finally into nothingness.

Wentworth was aware then that hands were holding him, helping him down from the precarious grip upon the rope; aware that Nita had been taken from his arms. He turned his head heavily, and looked into the grim, icy eyes of Laird. Only those eyes did not seem so cold now.

"Yon was a bonny sight," Laird said dourly. "A bonny trick, and a bonny way for a man like Munro to die!"

And Wentworth shook his head. From his pocket, he pulled out the slim platinum cigarette case and thumbed open its base. He pressed it down upon the railing where, a moment before, Munro had stood; afterword, there blazed there, *the seal of the Spider!* Bravado? Perhaps.

Laird had a gun in his fist, but as Wentworth watched, Laird turned that gun toward Warring and Hunter!

"Best you be going now, Spider," he said grimly. "The police will be here in a matter of moments. I'll hold these two hounds on the leash if they get too excited over the chase!"

Warring cursed Laird harshly and Hunter turned a heavy head. It was Hunter who spoke. "Don't be a damned fool, Laird," he said. "The Spider can burn down the city and I won't lift a hand to help catch him. By God, Spider, you're all man!"

Wentworth straightened, and managed a very formal bow.

"Gentlemen, I thank you!" he said.

It was all he could contrive. He staggered off down the bridge....

IT WAS not surprising that Richard Wentworth, when they found him in the battered truck that Munro had abandoned, should be pretty badly used up; or that his left hand had been fractured. But battered as he was, he insisted on going straight to Kirkpatrick when he heard of Munro's plunge, so that he could demand that the river be dragged.

"You can't be sure of that man's death!" he said flatly. "It's possible to hit the water right from that height, and survive!"

Kirkpatrick agreed... and Wentworth spent a week in the hospital before he could be arraigned in court.

Wentworth was his old dapper self when he appeared, and there was a contrite expression on his face.

"Your Honor," he said slowly. "I want to plead guilty... to charges of obstructing justice!"

The Judge glared down at him through a long minute. "I've very little patience with you high-living sybarites who should know better! Going around committing crimes for a thrill! You're a disgrace to your class!"

Wentworth said, meekly, "Yes, sir!"

"Have you had enough of this playing at being a detective?" the Judge demanded, leaning forward to peer over his spectacles, "or do you think a prison term would help to teach you to quit meddling with the sure processes of the law? The law always wins, young man! Justice will always prevail!"

Wentworth said, meekly, "Yes, sir!" The Judge grunted, leaned back.

"The sentence of this court," he said grumpily, "is that you shall...."

The door at the back of the court slapped open and Kirkpatrick entered.

"I wish to beg the court's pardon," he said, "for this intrusion. Dick, we found Munro's body in the river, and I was right. He was Maurice!"

Wentworth jerked about. "Are you sure? When I was his prisoner in the truck, I saw his right hand, and he had the seal of the Spider on its back!"

Kirkpatrick shook his head. "That's no good," he said. "This man had no right hand! There were some negatives—completely ruined!"

Wentworth shook his head. No, there was no proof yet that Munro was dead.

The Judge leaned forward. "Mr. Commissioner," he said. "Do you want to be fined for contempt?"

Kirkpatrick apologized hurriedly and withdrew, and the judge glowered down at Wentworth. "So they caught the man, in spite of your obstruction, young man! The court wishes to be lenient! The sentence is one year!"

Nita rose to her feet in protest.

The Judge glared at her. "Another interruption? Have you anything to say, young woman?"

"Plenty!" Nita snapped.

Wentworth said quietly, "It's all right, dear. After all I did obstruct justice!"

The Judge smiled suddenly. "I like your spirit, young lady, if not your good judgment. A year in prison, prisoner at the bar… *suspended!*" He chuckled. "But don't think it's going to be easy! In bed by ten o'clock every night. No drinking, and no carousing. No moving without permission. No leaving the jurisdiction of this court. You can't marry, and your companions will be rigorously supervised. If you associate with criminals, you serve the full term!"

Wentworth said meekly, once more. "Yes, sir. It serves me right… for obstructing justice!"

OPERATOR 5

- ❏ #1: The Masked Invasion — $13.95
- ❏ #2: The Invisible Empire — $13.95
- ❏ #3: The Yellow Scourge — $13.95
- ❏ #4: The Melting Death — $13.95
- ❏ #5: Cavern of the Damned — $13.95
- ❏ #6: Master of Broken Men — $13.95
- ❏ #7: Invasion of the Dark Legions — $13.95
- ❏ #8: The Green Death Mists — $13.95
- ❏ #9: Legions of Starvation — $13.95
- ❏ #10: The Red Invader — $13.95
- ❏ #11: The League of War-Monsters — $13.95
- ❏ #12: The Army of the Dead — $13.95
- ❏ #13: March of the Flame Marauders — $13.95
- ❏ #14: Blood Reign of the Dictator — $13.95
- ❏ #15: Invasion of the Yellow Warlords — $13.95
- ❏ #16: Legions of the Death Master — $13.95
- ❏ #17: Hosts of the Flaming Death — $13.95
- ❏ #18: Invasion of the Crimson Death Cult — $13.95
- ❏ #19: Attack of the Blizzard Men — $13.95
- ❏ #20: Scourge of the Invisible Death — $13.95
- ❏ #21: Raiders of the Red Death — $13.95
- ❏ #22: War-Dogs of the Green Destroyer — $13.95
- ❏ #23: Rockets From Hell — $13.95
- ❏ #24: War-Masters from the Orient — $13.95
- ❏ #25: Crime's Reign of Terror — $13.95
- ❏ #26: Death's Ragged Army — $13.95
- ❏ #27: Patriots' Death Battalion — $13.95
- ❏ #28: The Bloody Forty-five Days — $13.95
- ❏ #29: America's Plague Battalions — $13.95
- ❏ #30: Liberty's Suicide Legions — $13.95
- ❏ #31: Siege of the Thousand Patriots — $13.95
- ❏ #32: Patriots' Death March — $14.95
- ❏ #33: Revolt of the Lost Legions — $14.95
- ❏ #34: Drums of Destruction — $14.95
- ❏ #35: The Army Without a Country — $14.95
- ❏ #36: The Bloody Frontiers — $14.95
- ❏ #37: The Coming of the Mongol Hordes — $14.95
- ❏ #38: The Siege That Brought Black Death — $16.95
- ❏ #39: Revolt of the Devil Men — $16.95
- ❏ #40: The Suicide Battalion — $16.95
- ❏ #41: The Day of the Damned — $16.95
- ❏ #42: The Dawn That Shook the World — $16.95
- ❏ #43: When Hell Came to America — $16.95

G-8 AND HIS BATTLE ACES

- ❏ #1: The Bat Staffel — $13.95

CAPTAIN COMBAT

- ❏ #1: The Sky Beast of Berlin — $13.95
- ❏ #2: Red Wings For the Blood Battalion — $13.95
- ❏ #3: Low Ceiling For Nazi Hell Hawks — $13.95

ACE G-MAN

- ❏ #1: The Suicide Squad Reports for Death — $14.95
- ❏ #2: Coffins for the Suicide Squad — $14.95
- ❏ #3: Shells for the Suicide Squad — $14.95
- ❏ #4: The Suicide Squad in Corpse-Town — $14.95
- ❏ #5: Wanted–In Three Pine Coffins — $14.95
- ❏ #6: The Suicide Squad's Dawn Patrol — $14.95
- ❏ #7: Targets for the Flaming Arrow — $16.95

DUSTY AYRES AND HIS BATTLE BIRDS

- ❏ #1: Black Lightning! — $13.95
- ❏ #2: Crimson Doom — $13.95
- ❏ #3: The Purple Tornado — $13.95
- ❏ #4: The Screaming Eye — $13.95
- ❏ #5: The Green Thunderbolt — $13.95
- ❏ #6: The Red Destroyer — $13.95
- ❏ #7: The White Death — $13.95
- ❏ #8: The Black Avenger — $13.95
- ❏ #9: The Silver Typhoon — $13.95
- ❏ #10: The Troposphere F-S — $13.95
- ❏ #11: The Blue Cyclone — $13.95
- ❏ #12: The Tesla Raiders — $13.95

MAVERICKS

- ❏ #1: Five Against the Law — $12.95
- ❏ #2: Mesquite Manhunters — $12.95
- ❏ #3: Bait for the Lobo Pack — $12.95
- ❏ #4: Doc Grimson's Outlaw Posse — $12.95
- ❏ #5: Charlie Parr's Gunsmoke Cure — $12.95

THE MYSTERIOUS WU FANG

- ❏ #1: The Case of the Six Coffins — $12.95
- ❏ #2: The Case of the Scarlet Feather — $12.95
- ❏ #3: The Case of the Yellow Mask — $12.95
- ❏ #4: The Case of the Suicide Tomb — $12.95
- ❏ #5: The Case of the Green Death — $12.95
- ❏ #6: The Case of the Black Lotus — $12.95
- ❏ #7: The Case of the Hidden Scourge — $12.95

THE SECRET 6

- ❏ #1: The Red Shadow — $13.95
- ❏ #2: House of Walking Corpses — $13.95
- ❏ #3: The Monster Murders — $13.95
- ❏ #4: The Golden Alligator — $13.95

CAPTAIN ZERO

- ❏ #1: City of Deadly Sleep — $13.95
- ❏ #2: The Mark of Zero! — $13.95
- ❏ #3: The Golden Murder Syndicate — $13.95

RED FINGER

- ❏ #1: Second-Hand Death — $24.95